The Heart
has
Many Rooms

JEANIE WOOD

D.O.L.L.

WOMEN

book series

D.O.L.L.

Daughters of Love & Light
www.daughtersofloveandlight.com
Adelaide, South Australia
admin@daughtersofloveandlight.com

© Jeanie Wood 2022

ISBN: 9780645508604

Cataloguing-in-Publications entry is available from the National Library of Australia
http:/catalogue.nla.gov.au

First edition published 2022

Dedication

This book is dedicated to two beloved women who gave me life. To my mother, Marjorie McTigue, who is long gone but taught me how to be a strong woman. To my mother-in-law, Waveney Wood, who is also gone home, and taught me how to be a strong Christian woman. Their loving legacies live on from generation to generation.

'My Father's house has many rooms; if that were not so, would I have told you that I am going there to prepare a place for you?'

John 14:2

Chapter 1

1975

W arm for October,' the mauve-haired lady in the seat opposite remarked. The carriage bumpety-bumped along and they jolted from side to side like rodeo riders. Elizabeth caught a whiff of 4711 from a flapping hanky. Was the woman talking to her?

She nodded politely just in case. Was that Magic Silver White through the woman's hair? Her Mum should do that. Lift her spirits. Elizabeth could suggest it but it would probably get the luke-warm smile and the pallid wave.

'You look lovely and cool and fresh.' The train woman was smiling more this time.

'Thank you.'

'Off somewhere special?'

Elizabeth nodded. From the corner of her eye she could just make out the ancient, blackened bricks of the underground tunnels rushing past in the near-dark. The world was buzzing. The electricity of the tracks was running through her veins. 'Starting my first job.'

'How wonderful.' The woman raised her hand and primped her hair turning her head this way and that with the sway of the train. 'Nervous?'

Perhaps. There was the swarm of bees in Elizabeth's stomach. 'A bit. Mainly excited.' Her shoulders twitched.

Outside the dark was ebbing towards the half-light before the train emerged from the tunnels. They snaked around the last bend, out through the framework into Circular Quay Station. The black web of the Harbour Bridge flanked the cove on one side, painters hanging from it like baby spiders. On the other side, the Sydney Opera House rose, a blinding white bird, pluming itself beside the shore. Green and yellow ferries ploughed the deep blue-green water, gulls whirling in their wakes like sheaves of letters in a willy-willy.

Elizabeth stood, straightened her tight, white skirt, picked up her handbag and waved at her train friend.

'God bless, dear,' said the woman.

If she'd had a grandmother, Elizabeth thought she'd be like this. Was she a grannie ghost? The train trundled out of the station. No, she was real enough, chatting away now to the young man sitting on the seat she had warmed.

A bright day for a new start. Elizabeth trod onto the escalator, flying with excitement, ready to use all that Technical College training in interior decorating.

She walked up through the Rocks feeling sick with joy and fear all mixed together. Glancing sideways into the shop windows, she admired the new white suit and navy blouse setting off her much-maligned red curly hair. The leafy streets to the offices laced their light and shade over her head.

There it was. A discreet colonial home made into a business with an Art Deco sign. She

11

lingered outside for a little, gathering poise to walk into the building. Three deep breaths, a confident smile pinned on and she pushed through the doors. The scent of furniture polish and new fabrics made her stomach clench and heart gallop. A few more deep breaths and she sat perched on a chair as the receptionist with the plummy voice summoned Tracey Allen to the foyer.

'Make yourself comfortable,' said Tracey, 'Would you like a cup of tea?' and her face split in a friendly grin.

Thank you, but I'm fine.' What a lie. Elizabeth's tongue was stuck to the roof of her mouth. Knees wobbling. That tell-tale rise of blood-rush was staining her neck and ears. 'I love your office,' she said, really for something to say. Although, it was very glamorous with its Dali prints against the wallpaper, and the comfortable chairs and work table. Maybe she was a little naive – maybe more than just a little.

'I'm glad you approve,' Tracey said.

Elizabeth's stomach tumbled.

Tracey added, 'You're going to be spending a lot of time in here. I promise you'll work hard and learn to be meticulous and practical. I don't have to teach you to be creative, I've seen your portfolio.' She smiled and went on, 'My last assistant left suddenly because of a family issue, so I get to train you. I do hope you're ready to be taught. Let me show you around and introduce you to everyone. Then we can get started.'

Tracey proved to be a businesslike woman, as clever as she was artistic. Working for the firm for some years, she hoped to be offered a partnership in the near future. But for all her professionalism, she was fair, just, eminently approachable and a great mentor.

Over the ensuing months they became firm friends. Elizabeth learned to accept her criticism as constructive and to express her own creativity for her projects. Tracey would often take her out to view prospective projects for fresh ideas. Her praise was sparing and when she finally remarked about some drawings, 'These are good, in fact they're very good,' Elizabeth bought herself a new paisley outfit to celebrate.

There was just one problem in Eden. The bane of the women's existence was one of the partners, Warren Nicolls. He greeted men with a hearty friendliness and women with unnerving familiarity. The girls in the office seesawed between laughing him off and avoiding him like a snake. The male partners in the firm looked the other way and saw him as an extrovert and popular with clients. Elizabeth's approach was avoidance and Tracey tried to protect her from his growing attention.

She had enough problems at home. Brightened by the security the job brought, her mum seemed to have more purpose. She even tidied, cleaned, washed and cooked as she basked in reflected glory. As the year moved on, however she slipped back into depression and ill health. Warren was a petty irritation compared to homelife. When he asked Elizabeth to stay back and lend him a hand, she could say with all honesty that she had to be home early to cook tea for Mum, just to encourage her to eat a little more.

Tracey took Elizabeth out to lunch one day at a small restaurant to discuss the growing problem with Warren. 'Where's this affair leading?' she asked.

'I hardly think affair is the right word. He asks me, I say 'no' and he asks me again.'

Tracey's face folded into a frown. 'You know Warren's married. Be careful, Liz, he has more influence than I have. He's a dangerous enemy.'

'He's a snake.' They were both laughing but Elizabeth determined to lay low until he found some other prey.

Winter came suddenly to Sydney that year, with cold, persistent rain and the annual flu epidemic. Just as suddenly her mum's chronic bronchitis turned into pneumonia. One cold windy Friday she came home to find the doctor's car parked outside . Nausea rose as she put her key into the door. Her Mum carefully avoided the cost of having the doctor make a house-call.

She was propped up in bed, pallid as the pillow-slip. The doctor was bending over her listening to her chest, a worried expression on his face. He smiled gently and ushered Elizabeth out of the bedroom. 'She's very ill. I'm going to call an ambulance immediately and have her admitted to hospital. You pack a few of her things and try not to upset her.'

Sitting by her Mum's oxygen tent at the hospital were the longest hours she'd ever passed. She was barely aware of those that came and went as they waged war against the slow dying. Through one night, the next day and into the next evening, Elizabeth sat hunched by the bed. The staff would send her to have meals in the canteen. She would leave briefly, buy some food, eat a few mouthfuls and then push it away to return to her vigil. Her Mum finally gave up the battle in the early hours of the morning.

Elizabeth was numb. She walked away from the shell of her mother into a cold grey Sunday morning. Church bells tolled. Home was icy and empty. She lay on her bed in the flat, too drained to sleep until her aching body won and turned off her brain.

On Monday morning Elizabeth went to work as usual. Her face said it all and even Warren turned away from making a comment as she passed him in the passageway through the offices.

Tracey pulled her into her room. 'What on earth happened? You look dreadful.' When Elizabeth told her she was appalled. 'Why on earth are you at work today?'

'Where else do I have to go?' Elizabeth collapsed into one of the office chairs.

Tracey made tea, reorganised her appointments and took Elizabeth back to the house to help make the funeral arrangements.

Chapter 2

It didn't rain the day her Mum was buried. The sun shone bright on a perfect winter's day under a cold, blue sky. It could have teemed, for all Elizabeth cared. Her mum was gone. The sunshine had come too late to lift her mother's suffering. Tracey came. There was a soft tap on Elizabeth's shoulder, and she turned around, a surge of gratitude rising up from her frozen insides. Few other friends attended the service at the nearby funeral parlour and fewer still came to the muddy graveside at the family plot. But then Mum had kept herself to herself, as she said, all those years, and she was the last of her generation. Elizabeth would have liked to have told her stepfather, but she had no address for him. It would have been so easy to blame him for their misfortunes. But mostly she blamed the fickle sun appearing too late for her mum.

Back at work life marched on relentlessly, and little by little Elizabeth returned to the land of the living. Tracey helped her sort out her mum's things one Saturday, and they bundled up clothes and shoes, hats and bags and seemingly all that had been the person she loved, and gave them away to a local mission. Afterwards they shared coffee at a local café.

'Your mum didn't have many friends?' Tracey asked.

Elizabeth shook her head and shrugged. It was difficult to explain how her Mum had held people at a distance. 'I guess she was always a private person.'

Tracey looked at her expectantly. 'No other family then?'

'Just us.' A small sob escaped Elizabeth and she looked away, out the door to the people hurrying past in ones and twos and threes.

'What happened to your father?'

Maybe Elizabeth was born a private person too. Or maybe she learned it from her Mum.

'He died when I was twelve months old.' There it was. The rehearsed sentence her Mum had used so often. Whether it was truth or lie, Elizabeth was never really sure.

Tracey sipped her coffee thoughtfully. 'And there was never anybody else?'

How much could she say without betraying the stepfather she had loved as a father? Staring down into the cup, she was trying to piece together the fractured puzzle of her life.

'It's okay, Liz,' Tracey patted her hand, 'if it's too hard to talk, you don't have to. I just hate to see you so alone. I thought there might be family we could contact.'

Elizabeth watched as her tears plop plopped into the teacup like frogs in a pond.

Tracey offered her a clean, lacy hanky, but the dam had burst and a square of linen was no match for the flood. They sat there, Elizabeth bawling her eyes out in Tracey's embrace. Elizabeth noticed nobody. Tracey was her solidity in a world of swirling misery.

As she calmed and the sobbing subsided, Tracey ordered two more mugs of tea and some vanilla slices. 'Sugar's good for the soul,' she said. 'And vanilla slices are good for everything.'

That made Elizabeth smile a little.

'Do you want to tell me?' Tracey asked, and this time Elizabeth nodded.

She believed her Mum had suffered from depression most of her life. As a single mother with a baby she struggled until she married Elizabeth's stepfather. He was a lovely man and a wonderful father and they were happy when she was very young. 'He was the kindest man and I guess it wasn't his fault that he liked women. Mum must have been hard to live with but, as I grew up, I resented having to cover up for his girlfriends.'

She'd seen him once when she was out with some school friends. One of them stared across the road then asked, 'Isn't that your father over there with his arm around that woman?' She really didn't know what to say. She was caught between love for each of her parents - and she did think of him as her dad. When her mother found out, her reaction was amazing 'I'm the one he comes home to. This isn't the first and it won't be the last!'

Elizabeth's words were gushing out without discretion. It was like she was trying to explain Mum to herself as well as to Tracey.

Then there was the day he didn't come home. Just a note on the kitchen table, and an echoing emptiness in the unit. 'I've still got the birthday cards he sent me every year although my mum wasn't happy about them. I saw him in the street once and waved, but he turned and hurried away. Mum mostly talked about how much she'd sacrificed in 'putting up' with him for so many years when it was me that needed the father. *You never asked me*, I thought, but couldn't say.'

'So she locked herself away?'

'Yes. Lived on the pension. We were very careful. She was delighted when I did well at Technical College and came to work for you.' A secure position, she had said, and security was her byword. 'And it was great to have some more money coming in.'

'You cared for her for a long time,' Tracey remarked lifting her mug to her mouth.

'For ever.' An admission wrenched from the bottom of her being.

'Time to look after you now.'

And suddenly Elizabeth felt like she was released into the big black hole of nothingness.

'Work will help,' Tracey added.

'Thank you,' Elizabeth said, without knowing why she said it.

Tracey smiled and shook her head. 'Don't thank me yet. Wait until you see what I want you to do.'

There was little to keep Elizabeth home, her Mum haunted every room so she poured herself into the business. Tracey was a good friend, but she had her own life and, when day's end came, Elizabeth returned to her empty space. Her boss was involved with a colleague from another firm who was charming, thoughtful and already married. They both saw no wrong in the situation and Elizabeth began to throw off all her old ways and adopt a more cosmopolitan attitude to life.

The blankness at home drove her earlier to, and later at work - and more and more into the worrying presence of Warren Nicolls. His obsession grew daily and he lurked around every corner. Tracey would send her out on errands at the politic moment. But still he persisted.

Chapter 3

The first time Elizabeth saw Martin he was chatting to Warren in the foyer. Warren had, in his usual jovial and acquisitive way, stopped to greet a new face. She heard Martin say he had come in on his father's recommendation. Arms full of fabric samples, she passed and both heads turned.

'Take your eyes off her mate, she's mine,' Warren trumpeted. Martin smirked. Elizabeth fumed. Bad enough Warren's needling, without bringing his cronies in to join the game.

Martin, however, was a client too small for Warren's attention. Merely calling in at his father's insistence, he wanted to consult about his new house. The project had a stringent budget but, as the family were friends of the

Managing Director, it was accepted and eventually came to Tracey.

'I'm just overloaded with that hotel chain at the moment,' she said to Elizabeth. 'Maybe you could try your hand, with my approval naturally. After all it's not a very big house - you should do well with it.'

Excitement bubbled up under her ribs. Her own project.

It seemed Martin owned a growing hardware business in Campbelltown, to the South West of Sydney. He had become tired of first commuting from his parent's home, then renting a flat in the local suburb, and had decided to invest in a twenty-five-acre block between Liverpool and Campbelltown and build himself a house. The building itself was now finished but he was at a loss to know how to go about decorating and furnishing.

The first step was to visit the house and get a feel for it, and since Elizabeth didn't drive, Tracey made arrangements for Martin to pick her up from Liverpool Station the following Saturday around midday and visit the house.

Elizabeth's stomach felt like it had mozzies buzzing around, her limbs were stiff and twitchy, and her attention span was like that of a gnat. At last, she had her first project. Small, maybe, but it made the sun shine and the grief of the past winter lighter. She found herself smiling for no good reason as the train hummed along the rails.

Perhaps that attraction to Martin began on the station. There he was in jeans and a T shirt, a different person from the smooth operator in the foyer with Warren. Then he smiled, a genuine, sincere greeting. His dark brown hair flopped over his brow, his grey-green eyes crinkled and twinkled, his wide mouth lifted at the corners as he moved forwards. Inside Elizabeth, the lock opened and joy rushed up her body.

'Nice to see you again.' He shook hands formally, steering her out into the car park.

All she could do was grin.

'Good to have some time off,' he added

She nodded.

'Don't have much these days – still, it's exhilarating – success – and I don't really need much sleep!'

Elizabeth didn't have any idea what to say to that, so she smiled on and gazed out the car window as the city gave way to wide expanses of paddocks and hills.

Martin rambled on as they wound through the hills, pointing out local landmarks, interesting houses, the distant skyline of Sydney from one high ridge, livestock in paddocks, dams, practically anything to fill up the silence. Warren had hinted that Elizabeth was empty-headed but ambitious, but her rapt gaze on the countryside and absorption in his unending stream of information changed his perception.

'Why did you choose this district to build?' she interrupted the flow.

'I grew up surrounded by city streets and traffic. This looked so peaceful.' He stopped to think and the silence lengthened as he rounded a corner. 'I came out here to make a delivery to a customer one wintry day and the sun was setting just over that hill.' He nodded in the general direction. 'The whole ridgeline was on fire. All the trees were burnished with gold. After that I used to look in the Real Estate Agents in Campbelltown. One day there it was, my hill. It's great to be young and have the freedom to do what you want.' He grinned broadly, and turned into a gateway, along a dirt road around the side of a hill, and stopped.

The house was a revelation. From the road it was unimposing to say the least; just a facade with a door, a couple of windows and a double garage. As they walked through the entrance and into the foyer, the wide view beyond emerged. The pungent scent of new timber would linger in Elizabeth's memory of that first visit to the house. She would remember hearing her heels tap tapping down the steps and across the new wooden floor to the glass wall that lined the far side of the room. He drew open the glass doors and instantly she could feel the draw of the bush. A wide veranda overlooked paddocks with scattered gum trees, a creek, dams and in the distance the rolling hills. The house had been built into the contour of the ridge. It was an Lshape plan with the bed rooms spilling down the hill on one end and the main rooms along the ridge at the top ending with the garage. Lined with a terraced veranda, sometimes roofed, and in other places just beamed.

Its unity with the landscape was inspirational. Even the bricks and tiles on the roof seemed to melt into the surroundings. She turned to Martin, who was quietly waiting, and breathed, 'It's wonderful!'

He let out a sigh of relief but before he could say anything she dropped her carryall, sat suddenly on the floor, pulling her hair back out of the way, gazed up at him and cried, 'Now tell me what you would like, and I'll tell you how we'll do it.'

They sat cross legged in that light-filled room, and spoke of possibilities. It was probably not very professional to waste time this way, however it was Saturday, and her time to spend as she pleased.

'How did you get interested in decorating?' Martin asked.

'Well ... no, I can't tell you. You'll just laugh at me.'

'I promise I won't.' He poured his charm like a warm drink

'It began when I was very young. My dad – well my stepdad really – made me a dolls house. It was just a basic house, but I had such a great time painting walls, and making my own furniture. I used to redecorate regularly. Trying out colours and patterns and furniture. And I kept it up for years.'

He was smiling, not laughing, as promised. 'Wow, that's fantastic.'

'I used to hang around the newsagents and while all my school friends were reading *Dolly*, I was looking at magazines about houses. There weren't many around in those days – not like today.'

'You must have been meant to do it,' he grinned, 'born with a paintbrush in your hand.'

She nodded. 'I used to offer to help people decorate. Not many people'll let a child paint and wallpaper their walls. And we lived in a rented flat so that was a no, no.'

Then he laughed – and so did Elizabeth. Their hands touched as he helped her up from the floor, and electricity shot from fingertips to toes. Non-plussed, she looked away and wandered over to point out the window, ask about the countryside, and change the subject.

Eventually they wandered around the other unpainted rooms. Even the kitchen and the bathroom were still to be planned, and, as the shadows lengthened and Martin drove her back to the station, she was totally engrossed in making his house into a home.

And so the weeks danced by for Elizabeth. Tracey asked how she'd got the old spring back in her step and Elizabeth shrugged, but she knew. The fatigue that had dogged her since her mum died was gone. Saturdays were the only days when Martin could come out to the house. Those dreaded empty weekends were suddenly filled with purpose. He would pick her up early in the morning and she could work on her own 'til he returned from work at lunchtime. He took to bringing picnics to share on the panoramic veranda. Elizabeth drew careful and detailed plans and the time she worked on them probably far outweighed the firm's quote. But to sit in the sunlight, dreaming a home, was heaven. They found that their tastes were so similar that when he half mentioned an idea, she understood completely and was able to breathe life into it.

The day the planning was finally completed was drippy and drizzling. The trees dribbled crystal and trickling showers came and went. They spent the afternoon in the lounge where he had lit the fireplace for the first time. Sitting on the floor before the leaping flames, eating take-away Chinese, drinking wine, the two were suddenly so close. Neither was surprised by the intensity of the passion. There had been many times when their eyes had locked, hands touched, they'd brushed against each other, or even deliberately sat with legs pressed together, but now things were beyond control. Their coming together seemed an inevitability. He seemed surprised it was her first time but she urged him on and, as the pain passed and the ecstasy of climax gripped, it was as if the house beamed its benediction.

Martin drove Elizabeth all the way home that night, but she didn't invite him in, couldn't bear him to see the drabness.

'I can't see you tomorrow, my youngest nephew is being christened,' he said gently.

'It doesn't matter.'

He squinted in confusion. 'Would you like to come to the christening?'

To see him surrounded by his family would have left her more alone. 'No thanks.'

'I don't want to leave you like this.'

'I'm fine. I'm used to being on my own, you know.' Elizabeth opened the car door, jumped out, shut the door, waved and was up the steps and in the door before he could touch her again.

Chapter 4

Sunday was a blue day. Her mother's mantra haunted her. 'You can't depend on men. They only want one thing. Once they have it, they're done.' Her head was spinning like a merry-go-round but Elizabeth was determined to be independent.

By Monday her mind was made up. Somehow, she had got herself into this relationship that ended up in a one-night stand. She was not that sort of girl, and definitely not going to be naïve with this affair. It was a year since her first day. She could ask her for three weeks' holidays and resettle. Finish the project and then take off the next three weeks. First step was to present the completed drawings to Tracey for a final approval.

'I knew you could do it. These are inspired.' Tracey was glowing. 'They should be well within our client's means. I guess you deserve some time off after putting in all this effort, so if you work really hard this week and help me tidy up all my loose ends, of course you can have the time. Going somewhere exciting?' Tracey was peering at Elizabeth as she tried to control her traitorous face.

'No, I'm reshaping my life. First thing I'm ringing my landlord and giving notice on the old unit. Then I'm going to find somewhere fresh to live. These three weeks should give me enough time to give away or throw out everything around me and find somewhere to live where the sun actually shines.'

Tracey's eyebrows shot up. She was delighted, obviously the project had been just the shot to jog her trainee back to life.

Monday and Tuesday flew past with never ending industry. Martin invaded her thoughts constantly. Eyes shut and there was his smile, the smell of his aftershave, the taste his lips, the hardness of his body against hers. Each time the phone rang her stomach roiled with anticipation, but it was never him. Tracey's constant requests made the office frantic, packing and sorting the flat brought exhaustion each night.

Suddenly on the Wednesday afternoon her world flipped and all the brilliant plans began to unravel. Tracey was called to the country to troubleshoot on a project and left a long list of jobs to be completed. Elizabeth found herself working back, once again at the mercy of Warren Nicolls. The office was quiet and she was finishing off the final task for the day, bending over the planning table, when arms gripped her around the waist and she was pulled back against a stout body. 'You're such a tease.' He nuzzled her ear.

'Leave me alone.' She should have felt frightened, but all the emotions that had possessed her body exploded and she roughly pushed him off.

'Come on, everyone knows you like this.' He grabbed her again and squeezed until she thought she would break. Livid beyond reason

Elizabeth grabbed the nearest thing, a pair of scissors. Spinning in his arms she waved them about.

'I'll show you just how much I enjoy it!' She struck out blindly.

He ducked but the blade tip caught his cheek leaving a bloody gash. He yelled and backed away. 'You little bitch!' Blood dripped between his fingers as he pressed the wound.

'I told you to leave me alone.'

'Leave you alone?' He tried to leer and winced. Hysteria rose in her at his screwed-up face. 'Not on your life. Wait 'til I'm finished with you, I'm going to have you charged with assault.' He turned on his heel and stomped out of the office.

Collapsing into a chair, she shook. What on earth had possessed her to do such a thing? She could have killed him. Her rebel heart wished she had.

Fear hit like a brick wall as she passed out the glass front doors. Didn't he deserve it? What defence could there be if he had her charged. What would happen to the wonderful job? She passed the local pub on the way to the station. A board outside announced *Happy Hour.* A bit of Dutch courage was just the medicine.

Gulping down a drink she sat brooding, nursing the empty glass. Someone tapped her on the shoulder and she jumped.

'You're the last person I'd expect to find here!' exclaimed an excited voice, and there was Charlotte from Technical College.

'Well, what are you up to? Working? Or just spending money like me? That's right you're the worker and I'm the spender, I know!' she giggled.

Despite her misery, Elizabeth had to smile. Lottie never changed. They exchanged a quick hug,

'Not much.' Well, that was an outright lie. 'What are you up to?'

'I'm free-lancing.' Lottie screwed up her mouth. 'You can imagine how that impressed my father. He wants me to get a good solid job, but I told him I'm a free spirit.'

The two girls drifted out of the pub and down towards the Quay to share a bite to eat. The heavy weight Elizabeth had been carrying was beginning to lighten. Then Lottie asked about her Mum and she almost collapsed in the middle of Macquarie Street. Lottie led her friend over to the wall around the Botanic Gardens and they perched there as she sobbed. Lottie considered herself close enough. She thought she should have been told about Elizabeth's mother's death. All those years of training in keeping private, and Elizabeth had missed out on the comfort of a good friend.

Lottie for her part, came from a large, extended family who were always trying to *make her over in their own image*. Her clothes were no less original than her decorating designs and probably not to everyone's taste. But the affection she offered all far outweighed her eccentricity. Elizabeth wiped her face and gave her nose a hearty blow. Lottie took her arm from around her friend and grasped her hands.

'Better?' she asked.

Elizabeth nodded. The heaviness in her head was ebbing and crying seemed to have loosened the terrible tightness in her chest. She gulped in a deep breath.

'Let's go find some dinner,' Lottie suggested and towed Elizabeth off down towards the rippling harbour, its ferry lights flitting like fairies in the dusk.

She did feel better after some food. Her mum had always said she couldn't eat when she was depressed, and it must have been in Elizabeth's genes because in the last week she'd eaten very little. Having spilled her guts, so to speak, she had room for some food in them, joked Lottie.

'Anyway,' Elizabeth asked, 'what have you been up to?' Hopefully the conversation could be a little more positive. Lottie, as ever, was bubbling away with rebellion.

'I'm resting at present - as they say in the theatre. Dad's latest suggestion is that I go live in the bush with Grandma. She's getting frail and needs a companion. But, much as we love one another, we'd drive each other balmy. I'm too way-out for her tastes and I just can't stand the country life where nothing happens and everybody knows about it!' She grinned irrepressibly.

'Oh, Lottie, I really miss you - and our talks.' Suddenly the gloom entombed Elizabeth again, 'Give me your phone number and I'll ring you as soon as I'm in my new place.'

As they parted, they promised to see each other at least weekly.

'Chin up,' Lottie encouraged, 'it can't get any worse.'

Famous last words.

The following morning, Elizabeth forced herself to walk in to work head high and was relieved not to see Warren. Relief soon turned to horror when one of the young secretaries came in with the office gossip. Warren had been attacked and was in hospital. What to do? Who would listen? What would happen to the job? Remain calm, she told herself as her gut tightened around her brain. All she had to do was complete all the jobs Tracey had left. The day progressed and she sank into nausea. If only Martin would ring. No, never ask a man for help. Not even Martin.

Thursday was pay day and, in addition to the normal amount, Elizabeth received holiday pay. The train click clacked home and she resolved to make a clean break and leave the firm. After all, Tracey had warned there was nothing she could do about Warren, and he had said there was no future there. Why not leave now with all that was owing and start afresh somewhere completely new. She rang Lottie from home and, for once, surprised her friend.

'Do you think your grandmother would have me for a companion?'

Lottie chortled like a chook through the phone. 'You'd certainly be better at it than me. But what do you want to do that for? You've got a job, haven't you?'

'Not anymore I haven't. I need to leave. And I need a place to go where I can't be found.'

'Okay,' said Lottie slowly, 'you're on the run.' She breathed deep into the phone, obviously thinking hard. 'Look, I'm sure she'll love you. And it might be just the thing after losing your mum like that. You might even convince her to do something with that terrible old house. Chuck out some of the rubbish. Dad would love that. He thinks he's going to have to clean it out when she dies.'

'Really?'

'Yes, really. She told him that's her plan. To make her kids do all the work.'

Elizabeth laughed, and laughed, and laughed – quite hysterically – and wondered what she was getting herself into.

Lottie rang her father, who rang her grandmother, who rang Lottie back. Elizabeth was to take the train out to Cowra the following evening.

She stayed up all night packing what was left. First thing the next morning the Salvation Army came and picked up all the left overs and by five o'clock that night she was on the train with all her possessions packed in a tea chest in the luggage compartment, a new life before her. A letter of explanation and apology had been sent to Tracey along with her resignation.

The train chugged out through the suburbs, past the sprawl, passing new housing estates and then through the mountains, rosy with sunset. All memories or regrets were pushed down or put aside, not to be considered for the pain they brought.

Elizabeth fled Sydney, future forsaken, ambitions abandoned, and bridges merrily aflame.

Chapter 5

The warmth of the day had drifted away and it was a cool, cloudless night, as she stepped out of the train onto the country station. The moon had set as the train travelled across the plains but the burning stars were so bright the countryside was clearly etched in grayscale. A few other passengers stepped off the carriage and were met by people who smiled and hugged and kissed them, or shook hands. The train pulled out, bound for further west and Elizabeth plonked onto her tea chest beneath a dim pool of light, hugging her suitcase.

A middle-aged man appeared unexpectedly at the gate, said 'G'day' to the station master and then approached. 'You staying with old Annie?' That threw her. Lottie had never mentioned her grandmother's name.

'I'm not sure. Is her name Mrs. Webster?'

'Yeh.' He looked doubtfully at the tea chest. 'Can't take that. Too big.'

'Perhaps we could leave it here and I could hire someone to bring it over in a truck?'

'Old Annie'll know what to do.' Suddenly she had an image of an elderly lady pushing the tea chest down the road. 'Oi, Jack,' the station master put his head out, 'can we put this in the storage area?' The two men shoved the box into the station goods area and nodded knowingly at each other. They had no doubt Old Annie would fix it.

Elizabeth climbed into the waiting cab, and it drove sedately through the sleepy town. 'Not one of Annie's.'

Was it a question or a statement? 'Why do you say that?'

'That hair!'

She let the hair comment pass. He drove down the main street, past the locked shops and the post office, the police station, empty footpaths with darkened houses, beside huge shady trees that lined the wide streets. They finally pulled up outside a weatherboard house surrounded by a wide veranda.

Ushering her through the wire gate and up the three steps onto the porch, the taxi driver knocked with a great brass knocker on the solid timber door three times. A voice rang through the timber, 'Righto. Hang on. Hang on. I'm not deaf. Don't knock the door down.' He smiled knowingly and waggled his head. There were shuffling footsteps on the other side of the door before it swung open. Small, brown and wrinkled like a gumnut baby, was the first impression. 'Well, come in child, come in. Don't let the flies in. Pay Les - don't add extra this time Les – then let's get you settled.'

'G'day Annie, how are you? Keeping well?' Les pulled change out of his pocket and Elizabeth felt the warm money on her cold palm.

'Fine, fine Les - I'm running in the gallops come Saturday.' They both laughed. 'How's Shirley and the kids?'

'Fighting fit - you might say.' Annie closed the door behind him.

Her faded eyes sparkled. 'Les has four boys and their lovely kids, but "fighting fit" describes them most days.' She slowly led the way through the house, redolent of the past. Mixed together were photos and ornaments and furniture, the bygone and the present - a lifetime or two or more. Suddenly and completely drained, Elizabeth was overcome by the strangeness of the place and the weight of its history. The room at the back of the house was a large kitchen where a fuel stove burnt merrily and a kettle chortled away on the hob.

Annie sat her down in a chair and served scrambled eggs and tea. She kept up a stream of dry comments. Later Elizabeth could remember smiling at these, but not the words. Before she knew it, she was tucked in a high old bed, wondering just who was supposed to be doing the caring, as she plummeted into a deep, dreamless sleep.

Magpies trilled outside the window. Sun filtered through the old lace curtains, casting weird patterns across the chenille bedspread. Pink rosebuds on the wall paper, pink fluff under her hands on the bedspread, the fragrance of the pink roses in a vase on the antique dressing table. She was suddenly awake – and completely lost. Sitting up in bed she plopped her feet on the worn boards beside the bed and felt rooted to reality. Like an electric current, memory came flooding back: taxi, train trip, resignation, Warren's accusations, Martin. Disappointment was like ashes in her dry mouth. That's right, she was supposed to be the housekeeper. Pulling on jeans and a blouse, and rapidly brushing and tying back her hair, she raced down the dusty runner in the hallway.

'Morning, Sleeping Beauty.' Annie cracked a grin.

'Sorry, Mrs Webster, I'll be up earlier tomorrow. Heat rose up her neck but Annie waved away the apology.

'I don't sleep much these days. Too hard to get comfortable. But I stay in bed just in case I can drift off for a bit.' The old woman patted her hand. 'I looked in on you when I finally crawled out of bed at seven but you were still dead to the world. Seemed a pity to wake you up. I figured you must need your rest. Pour yourself a cuppa.' She pointed to the teapot in the middle of the table covered in a knitted teddy bear tea cosy. 'My granddaughter made me that.' She laughed. 'Said my old one I made when I was her age had too many stains on it. I didn't mind the stains. Every one brought back a conversation with somebody I loved.' She wheezed a little. 'Some of them you could repeat – not all of them.' And then she laughed out loud.

Elizabeth's tension was subsiding, sliding away like a satin curtain gently falling.

'What do you like for breakfast? I've got toast and butter and lots of jams – all homemade. Not by me these days, but they're my recipes. Or there's vegemite. Help yourself. They're all in the pantry over there.'

'Thank you.' Elizabeth went exploring in the huge walk-in cupboard. Then thought again. 'Can I get you anything?' She was supposed to be the carer.

Annie shook her white curls. 'I'm not useless you know, just a little stiff in the mornings. And I don't need a keeper, just someone to do the jobs I hate doing. Like cleaning and dusting. My girls offer to do it but they have enough to do and they aren't as young as they were. A farm wife means a busy life - or you could say a farm life means a busy wife.' She cackled again at her own wit.

Elizabeth took her toast back to the table along with a pot of marmalade and sat down. 'Did you live on a farm?'

'Yeah. Worked hard all my life both in town and on the land. Now it's my kids' turn. And they insist I need a looker-after. I told 'em, by the time your past ninety you need someone to do what you don't want to do. But if I want to make myself a cuppa that's my business. Right?' She peered aggressively across the table and added, 'And I'm Annie, Don't call me Mrs. Webster, I keep looking for Gus's mother, God rest her soul!'

Elizabeth couldn't help smiling and agreeing. 'Your house is lovely,' she said, gesturing around the sunny kitchen.

Annie relaxed. 'Well, it was, but it's a bit shabby nowadays and beyond me. I just don't have the energy. Not that I'd let on to the family.

They'll probably do it up when I'm dead. I hope someone wants all the relics.'

That stumped Elizabeth. Lottie was the only one of the family she knew. If she could offer some comfort to this proud old woman.

'It belonged to my mum and dad,' Annie went on. 'They owned the town bakery for thirty years 'til the supermarket opened and started bringing bread in from out of town. Still they lived on in this house for many years and died within a fortnight of each other.' Her watery eyes filled.

Elizabeth smiled and nodded and basked in the familiarity of the old woman's sharing. She rambled on about the history of the town, not told as instruction, but living, breathing stories of the present and the past and her family's part in it. The kitchen was full of sunlight, dust motes dancing, a dripping tap rainbow, the dull gleam of the old slate floor, enveloping them in possibilities.

Annie surprised her by snapping back to the present with a practical discussion on Elizabeth's employment. The amount she offered, of course, was much smaller than a decorator's wage, even a cadet. It was as much as she could afford and, with full board, would be quite enough. Elizabeth felt uncomfortable even taking the money. She vowed she would save and start again.

'Can you drive?' Annie suddenly asked.

Elizabeth shook her head as she carried the dishes over to the sink. 'I've never had the opportunity.'

'Well then that's the first thing we have to fix. You need a car out here. Leave that for later.' She nodded at the washing up. 'Follow me.' Out they traipsed through the back door. Spring was in the air and the house grounds were rimmed with fruit trees laden with fragrant blossom, crimson, pink and white. The side of the house stood in a bank of azaleas, old fashioned bushes falling over each other with the weight of their blooms. They stood against the fruit blossom colours with a myriad of purples and mauves and all the shades of pinks. Bees swarmed to drink in the nectar, but Annie never stopped in her eagerness to share her secret. A kookaburra gave full throat as she threw open the garage door and with a flourish revealed a gleaming blue Austin.

Annie shuffled around to the door, stumbled in, and backed it out into the driveway like a professional.

She wound down the window and scowled. 'They won't let me drive any more. Refused to renew my licence. Apparently, my reflexes aren't quick enough. I told them throw a punch and I'll show you how good my reflexes are. You know what they said? As if anyone would want to punch you. But they still wouldn't renew it.' Disgust and disappointment waved across her face. 'I need to be able to get around so I'll get one of my grandsons to teach you. That should grey your hair a bit.' And that was evidently, that.

The car was in very good condition, kept safe to drive by yet another grandchild. It had only ever been a *lady's* car and was hardly used. Annie's grandson John took on the task of turning the city pedestrian into a driver. He was possessed with a strange sense of humour. Every afternoon, rain or shine he arrived at 4.30 and gave the town it's evening's entertainment. They began by driving around the block.

He was not explicit enough, Elizabeth complained. What did come first, slowing down or changing gear? Hitting the brake or hitting the clutch? And why was third gear always where it shouldn't be. They mastered the home block in the first week and then John suggested they take an unfamiliar turn into the next street.

'No, I'll just keep going around here, thank you.'

'In that case we'd better move the shops and the relatives into this block, eh?'

'There's no need for sarcasm.' Teeth clenched.

'Not being sarcastic. Just realistic.'

Elizabeth graduated to the further world around the town. Everywhere people raised a greeting hand as they drove past and John would return the salute. Elizabeth gripped the wheel like a chimp on a jungle gym, and focused on the road.

They moved on to bumpy country roads.

'Gee, you missed that one,' John murmured as they avoided a pothole.

Once again, she was grinding her teeth. 'Happy to please.' Then, suddenly, she was laughing out loud.

'So you *can* laugh. I wondered.'

Elizabeth could feel herself relaxing and no longer regarding driving as taming a wild animal. John talked about his job at the local vehicle dealership. His tales of car sales were hilarious. At present, he said, he was free of entanglements. That made her feel a little shy. It suggested a closer relationship and she was definitely not up to anything close. She kept it light and fun and when he finally invited her on a date, she was much too busy looking after Annie.

Over that time, Annie and Elizabeth were working through the old house. Room by room, the older woman gave directions and the younger woman supplied the elbow grease. They gave the place a much-needed and thorough clean. The old furniture gleamed once more and the floors looked fresh and clean. Annie swore the old curtains would disintegrate, so, rather than a wash, they were hung out in the sun and given a good shaking. Ideas for restoration crowded

Elizabeth's mind and often at night, or when Annie was having her cat nap, she would take out her sketch pad and plan the rooms in different ways, restored to what they had been in their glory days.

Annie hated shop bread and insisted that Elizabeth learn how to bake. 'Never bought it when I could still knead. You know what Neville said?' Neville was a grandson who grew wheat and made small quantities of his own flour. 'He wouldn't give me any more. They think I'm too old and arthritic.' She held up her nobbled, twisted fingers. Neville had a point. They reached an agreement with the family that Elizabeth would do all the hard work if they gave Annie some stone-ground flour. The yeasty fragrance of newly baked bread once more haunted the house.

The family were all there to be seen in the photo gallery. On the mantle-shelf rested portraits of Annie's children beneath their father's stern, uniformed gaze. On the sideboard stood pictures of weddings and grandchildren. On the dresser brightly coloured photos of the grandchildren's marriages and their offspring marched in ranks. Annie was the matriarch. Each of her family separately prized. And each one visited Annie as soon as humanly possible to check the new girl's credentials. They came politely, pumped her unmercifully and left seemingly satisfied. Each night Elizabeth fell, tired and fulfilled, into her high bed and snuggled under the pink chenille bedspread.

And then it was marmalade making time. Annie swore that finely slicing the fruit would be good for her arthritis. The old house was bursting with the springtime flavour of orange and lemon and grapefruit. 'Gotta clear away the last of the winter crop - give the blossoms a chance.' John found Elizabeth up a tree when he came a little early to have tea and helped her down.

'Ready to take your driving test?' he asked.

Fresh bread, marmalade, tea and panic was overwhelming. 'I'll never do it!'

'Of course, you will,' Annie was bubbling over with confidence, 'I've had a word with Our Wee Jock.'

Jock MacMillan the town cop had come to visit before. At a burly six foot four and sixteen stone, he still carried the name his grandmother had assigned him. 'Not bribery!' Elizabeth cried, horror replacing panic.

'Pull yourself together girl. It's not the guillotine – just a driving test.' Annie spoke with eyewitness authority. Where was the knitting and cackling?

'Yeah,' added John with half a smile. 'You know the route – around the block, up the main street, down Bumpty Road and reverse park in front of the cop shop.'

'I feel sick,' Elizabeth whispered and they both laughed. But she really did.

Our Wee Jock gently took her through her test without hesitation. It was hard not to laugh at him trying to extricate his frame from Annie's little car. However, he treated the antique with due respect. So Elizabeth bit back the hysterics building from her gut, and returned home to Annie.

Nothing could contain the old lady's delight - she had her wheels back and, in the next fortnight, no relative was left unvisited. Elizabeth's confidence improved considerably as they toured at tortoise speed around the district's back roads. Annie liked to take in the scenery and urged a sedate pace. They meandered peacefully out to the farms, along dirt tracks lined with huge old gums leaning together in archways like old women gossiping. Every shade of green pulled at Elizabeth's creative heart. They paused by wooden fences around paddocks holding in ponderous cattle with skittish calves or bounding new lambs guided by ewes. Their favourites were the foals frisking around on their spindly legs and nuzzling into their mother's sides.

Annie would insist on taking something baked. 'Never go empty handed,' she said. 'Food's a great way to get to know people. I always think confession is sweeter over a piece of Victoria Sponge.'

Elizabeth's mother would have been horrified, always keeping herself to herself. They'd never visited anybody. Elizabeth realised she had blurted it out, without a piece of the persuasive Victoria sponge.

'Poor her,' said Annie, patting her on the knee. 'She really missed out, didn't she?'

Elizabeth nodded, eyes on the road.

'Just as well you came to me. Not only can you learn how to cook, you can practise visiting and being neighbourly.'

Elizabeth smiled, still eyes on the road.

'And how to get the gossip too,' Annie added.

And then they were both laughing.

Chapter 6

One morning, as they were putting the loaves in the oven, Annie baldly stated, 'Don't you think you should see the doctor, Liz dear?'

Elizabeth flopped into the chair and stared at her blankly.

'Do you want to talk about it?' Annie added

The floodgates burst and tears waterfalled down.

'That's right, a good cry always helped.'

'I..don't,..want...to ...be...pregnant..'

'You know,' said Annie quietly when Elizabeth's sobs subsided. 'I remember when Gus went away. I waved him off with my best white lace hanky. He was so proud, proud of himself saving his country for his wife and seven kids. I'd be right. The older boys could help. Herbie must have been conceived the night before he left. We obviously weren't careful enough. By the time my poor frail Herbie was born his dad was dead - gone with all the other Light Horsemen lost at the Dardanelles. The kids were proud their dad was an Anzac and so was I - but he should have seen them grow up. I didn't want to be pregnant either. But the Almighty had other plans for me. And He gave me the strength to cope.'

The long-gone tragedy stood like a beacon in grey future. Annie had seen suffering in her lifetime and had overcome. Perhaps there was a way.

'Feeling better?' Kind, faded eyes peered into hers and Elizabeth began to feel stronger. Annie offered an old lacy handkerchief, and Elizabeth blew her nose and nodded. 'Let's make a nice cuppa. Then you and I can have the little talk you've been wanting.'

They had that conversation Elizabeth didn't know she'd been wanting. With a warm cup held firmly between her slowly steadying hands, she told Annie about her mum. Guilt welled up inside – as if she was somehow to blame for her mother's misery. 'Perhaps if it hadn't been for me, she would have left my stepfather – or never married him in the first place.'

Annie declared this to be nonsense and no concern for a well-meaning daughter. 'You did your best. Be content with that.' When it came to the part about the job and Warren's role in the resignation, Annie's eyes blazed. 'I know what it's like,' her lips tight, 'it wasn't easy for young widows after the war. Women on their own have always been easy targets.'

Talking about Martin was more difficult. *One-night-stand* kept whirling around in her head and Elizabeth gripped the cup, striving for words to describe their time together. 'You were lonely,' Annie said, 'and he was kind. I'm sure he was a lovely young man, but he should have been more responsible. Don't you think you should let him know he's going to be a dad?'

What to say? Would he want to know? Elizabeth's upbringing told her, no, he wouldn't want the responsibility. There was also no way she was going back to a place Warren Nicholls held power. She begged Annie to forget the father. A woman was quite capable of bringing up a child. Annie was living proof of this. She had worked it out as she went. Annie shook her head but agreed she would not talk about the baby's father to anybody.

'I'll ring young Doctor Hooper and make an appointment for you. He's discreet and a good doctor. Now let's find you a wedding ring.' Despite protests, Annie dragged Elizabeth into the bedroom and started digging in her jewellery box. 'Ah, here it is. It belonged to my mother. I'm sure she'd love you to have it. After all it's just sitting in a box.' She pushed the ring up the fourth finger. 'Good fit. It'll stop any gossip – although no-one would dare say much about me and mine.'

Elizabeth's heart swelled with surprise and gratitude and relief that she belonged. She looked into Annie's bleary eyes and inclined her head in silent agreement.

The old ring was engraved with leaves still clear after all the years. 'She had skin trouble, so she only wore it to go out. Not like me.' Annie held up her hand with her narrow ring caught firmly on the papery skin between swollen knuckles. 'Tell them that's why you don't wear it often – because of eczema. Skin and hair like that, makes sense.'

Young Doctor Hooper was at least sixty, pragmatic and kindly. He confirmed the early pregnancy and made arrangements for regular visits and to book her into the hospital. When he asked about a husband, Elizabeth simply said, as Annie had coached her, they were separated. He asked no more questions. 'If you have any problems, come and see me straight away.'

Her mother had always condemned unmarried mothers, but Annie was of a different mould. 'Bad girls don't have babies. I always thought, There but for the grace of God go I. Anybody could be in your position.' She smiled at a memory of long ago. 'You have a home here for as long as you like. Take your time. Don't make any decisions right now.'

A few days later Elizabeth's mind was made up. Pulling weeds from beneath the fruit trees, the scent of grass and earth in her nostrils, she found herself saying. 'I'd like to stay here after the baby's born, if that's okay with you.'

Annie beamed, age lifting off her lined face.

'And I'm not going to adopt it out. I want to keep it. You raised your kids on your own, why can't I?' Elizabeth had another thought. 'Then we could get on with fixing this place up.'

Annie leaned forward from the garden chair and drew Elizabeth up into her ropey arms. 'I'm glad you've come to a decision. And just in case, I've spoken to George. He said he can start the painting in three weeks, so we'd better get moving. After all, if we want a nice clean house for this baby, we don't have long.' Delight swept over Elizabeth. Here was a project she could lose herself in.

Chapter 7

As her waist expanded, Elizabeth's lethargy contracted. She was ever truly sick – as Annie declared she had been – just constantly tired and a little nauseous from hunger. Annie made sure they napped together and ate regularly. This world was far removed from the modern bustle. Elizabeth's art, profession, and former concerns seemed distant now this new life was expanding daily. Annie had a wisdom born of eternal hopefulness and her encouragement urged the younger woman through the early days.

Christmas came and they celebrated at Annie's church and then a huge lunch out at the family farm. Lottie had sent a Christmas card announcing she would be skiing in Switzerland this Christmas. On a scorching Christmas day, this news was met by the family with scant regret and knowing humour. Most of her cousins said they missed her jokes but not her being the Family Organiser. Annie announced the coming baby in her usual matter-of-fact fashion. She had schooled her offspring well in tolerance and, if they discussed it, they did so away from the Christmas Pudding, or even the Victoria Sponge. They offered Elizabeth nursery furniture and promised hand-me-downs. It seemed she had become a member of the clan. They were universally delighted with Annie's new lease on life. She was eating and sleeping better and had plenty to occupy her hands and her mind. And then there was the house restoration.

At night, the two women would sit together in the kitchen, Annie in her favourite chair and Elizabeth at the table, first drawing plans of the rooms and then discussing how the house had been when it was first built. Annie relished the opportunity to share memories of her childhood in the house and the style of each space. The heat of January saw them dreaming away together, planning an autumn renovation.

When the colours were chosen, they visited the local drapers and borrowed catalogues to find matching fabrics. Annie would show their choices to her family, challenging them to object. The family was universally happy that this mammoth task was being taken on by someone else, and saw it as a scheme that kept Mum busy and gave her the gift of anticipation.

The weather cooled, the painter and paperer arrived and the project was off and running. Six busy weeks later the house was restored to its original federation feel. As far as possible they kept to the original mellow colours with new flowery, Victorian paper in the bedrooms. A compromise was neutral-coloured carpets instead of the original polished wooden flooring so Annie wouldn't slip and break a bone. Elizabeth worked in a frenzy, running up the curtains on the old Singer sewing machine. John came around to help hang the curtains as he refused to allow either woman to set one foot on the ladder.

'You're a pair of old hens, fussing over one another,' John laughed – and they nodded like the chickens pecking in the next-door coop.

John had made his quiet presence felt recently. 'I feel responsible for inflicting you on the highway system. Have to make sure you stay in line.' His eyes twinkled.

Elizabeth liked John. In fact, in the emotional months leading up to the birth, their closeness had become stronger than mere affection. She loved him like the big brother she'd always wanted. Someone to joke around with and ask for advice. Annie looked on speculatively as he teased and got back as good as he gave. Thank goodness John never seemed to want to take it further. It was as if there was an imaginary line drawn, cutting off any possibility of romance. As if Elizabeth belonged to someone else. Maybe she did. She might have been dreaming of renovation during the daytime, but Martin haunted her sleep. She would wake with the feeling of his hand on her hip, or his lips on her mouth, or the faint whiff in her nostrils of new sawn wood that he had carried on his clothes. *None of that*, she'd remind herself, *it's only all this work on the house that's stirring him up. Go away.* She would say, sometimes out loud, and Annie would call back, 'Are you talking to me, you know I can't hear what you say from another room.'

See, she'd inform her ghost, *you're not needed. I'm perfectly all right.* And she was. Mostly.

When the house was all finished, Annie was like a kid with a new toy. They would sit in the kitchen drinking tea, admiring all the new conveniences. Annie was smitten with her dishwasher. 'My old Mum would have killed for one of those things. Fancy a magic cupboard where you stack your dirty dishes, fill it up, turn it on and hey presto, the dishes are done.'

The federation look was still there and they'd even found somebody to clean and repair the one thing she refused to change – her kitchen range. 'You wait 'til the dead of winter,' she declared, 'it makes the whole house cosy and you can cook in the oven and on the top.' They agreed however, that the electric stove was perfect for summer.

Sitting watching TV in the lounge one early March night, Annie suddenly said. 'I think you should sign up for mothercraft classes at the hospital clinic. Jenny runs them. She says they're great for first timers.'

'Does she?' Jenny was a relative in some way. Where did she fit into the mosaic of Annie's family life?

'Yeah. Didn't have 'em in my day. I wish they had. It's a bit of a shock first time round. The birth and all that. And then when you bring 'em home, you're trying to work out what's making the baby cry. Here's Jenny's number.' She produced a paper scrap from her brunch coat pocket and put it into the young woman's outstretched hand.

Elizabeth knew very little about babies and even less about childbirth so the classes proved invaluable. Most women brought an embarrassed husband. Elizabeth brought Annie. 'Wanna see if it's any different from my time,' she said. 'The only advice I had was to be sensible and do what the nurse told me to do.'

'Has it changed any?' 'Elizabeth asked after the first class.

Annie curled up her lips and her head waved from side to side. 'Maybe. They seem to talk a lot more medical stuff than we heard. All those pictures – fascinating. And all that panting. I don't think I ever did that.'

They laughed, 'What did you do?' Elizabeth slowly turned the last corner to home.

'I moaned a bit, I guess, and wondered how the hell I'd ended up back doing it again. So I yelled at Gus. But he was outside so he couldn't hear me, drinking beer with his brothers mostly.'

'A different world then.' The car was in the driveway and Elizabeth pulled on the brake, and turned the engine off.

Annie nodded. 'It's a long time ago, and mine were all born at home. We had a local nurse that brought all the babies around here into the world. My sisters would come and help too. Only got the doctor if something went wrong.'

'Did you ever call the doctor?'

She nodded. 'When Herbie was born, we both nearly died. The placenta came first. So they brought the doctor then.'

Elizabeth cried out and Annie took her hands. 'You'll be fine,' she said. 'I'm not letting anything happen to my girl.'

They embraced.

'Steady there,' Annie mumbled. 'You don't want to break me while I'm still useful.'

The family were amazing. Every time one of them paid a visit, they would bring something lovely for the baby. Often these were home-made with love. Annie ferreted through the garage and found the original cradle she had used for her children. John took it away, rubbed it back and returned it beautifully painted in a creamy white. The granddaughters unearthed their supply of maternity clothes and brought them over for a try-on. Annie had also been teaching Elizabeth to knit. Together they produced the loveliest jackets and bootees for the baby.

With the rocker and the baby clothes in the original nursery the house felt full again, waiting to fulfil its original purpose. They often sat in the nursery and one day, Annie's eyes clouded over with tears. 'You know, Liz dear, if I could go back, I wouldn't change one moment of my life – just relive some of the loveliest bits. Like when I had my first baby and I laid him in that cradle. Yes, that would be one of them. The nine months is all worth it when you finally hold that dear little person in your arms.'

Kate came late. It was a frosty June night when the painless contractions suddenly slid into agonising spasms. Feeling uncomfortable all day without knowing what the ache meant, Elizabeth suddenly understood. Annie summoned John who drove her to the hospital. So much support, but when it came to the moment, with loving Annie and reliable John, waiting at home, there was just her and Kate. The nursing staff and the doctor were kind but she missed her mother terribly in those sterile, Spartan surroundings. It seemed like a primal yearning, going back to far memory.

'You should have ten, the way you did that,' joked the sister when it was finally over.

Elizabeth was too stunned to answer. The loneliness and the pain had left her silent and shaking. Kate lay wrapped in a warm rug, against her breast, blinking at the bright world. From the folds of the blanket, below her bright hair, stared Martin's eyes.

Naturally, Annie, was their first visitor, driven to the hospital by the ever-reliable John. She brought Kate's first pink frilly dress, wrapped in tissue. 'I guessed it was a girl.' Her lined face settled into a smug smile. 'Think you're clever, don't you! Well, you are. She's just beautiful.' The two women held each other while John grinned and took photos.

The day came when Kate lay in the white cradle, her hair bright against the white sheets and the Victorian cosiness. Elizabeth kept her beside her bed for ease at night, and lay listening to her breathe and snort and suck her little rosebud mouth in her sleep. Those cold, cold nights she would nurse Kate to her breast in the rocker by the old range and imagine her own mother nursing her. It changed her view. Now her mother was a woman who had done her best in her own way, locked in a view of the world that kept out others, unable to cut the cord binding her daughter. Elizabeth wondered if she would feel like that about this little person, and swore to encourage her to be independent.

Annie loved to watch the baby feed and sleep and knew how to offer comfort in those early, insecure weeks. 'You never lose your touch,' she declared. After the first couple of months, Kate settled down and contentedly fed and slept. 'You think you're doing everything right, don't you? I thought that with my first two, they did everything right. It was the third one that broke all the rules. She cried night and day for the first nine months. You've met my Louise – still talks all the time, just like her daughter Lottie. Likes to whinge too. So, make the most of this little one. What a good girl you are.' She tickled Kate's chin to make her laugh. Kate was the adored focus of our household. And if she looked like Martin, the pain was long gone.

As winter thawed into spring and spring blossomed into summer, Kate developed into a long-limbed, serene child. She began to sleep through the night, enjoyed her food, and her bright curls kept growing, so Annie would tie bows in her hair. There was a 1920s Pears Soap picture book of infants in her bedroom and Annie swore Kate fitted right onto the page with the rosy, curly-haired, timeless tots. 'My lovely, my lovely,' Annie would croon and rock her back and forth in the old rocking chair they had moved into the sunshine on the trellised veranda. Kate rewarded Annie by replying, 'Nan, Nan, Nan.' So Annie became Nannie. As Kate learned to crawl, the first chilly nights of autumn made them rug her up in old fashioned overalls. She now spent most of her time exploring the old house, finding long-forgotten treasures, and getting caught behind furniture. Annie was delighted, finding amusement and pleasure in every passing stage.

As Kate became a toddler, it was obvious she loved to please. If she was told not to do something, she rarely repeated it. Books were her favourite pastime. She would sit next to Annie for hours as the old lady read to her and talked about the pictures. Kate learned to make all the animal sounds and repeated them from her car seat as they toured around the neighbourhood. Dogs were her favourite and would always say 'Ah, puppy,' very lovingly to any dog.

Some of Annie's family questioned why Elizabeth never went away on holidays.

'You are entitled to them, you know,' forthright Louise declared, silencing Annie with a halting hand.

'I don't need a holiday, thanks, I'm perfectly happy here.' Elizabeth answered firmly

'I told you so,' snapped Annie. Obviously, this had been discussed.

'But you must be owed some,' Louise persisted.

'I don't want any. I'm happy where I am.'

'Leave her alone,' said Annie. And then changed the subject directly. 'Anyway what's Lottie doing with herself these days?'

'Oh,' answered Louise, looking annoyed but resigned. 'You know Lottie. She's still in London. She's got a big contract with a hotel over there. Says she'll be home for Christmas.'

'Did you ask her which Christmas,' Annie laughed.

Louise screwed up her lips at her mother, then laughed along.

Elizabeth rose quietly and took the teapot out to make a fresh pot. Kate was chortling away in her cot after her afternoon sleep and she lifted her out and into her arms.

Kate threw her little arms around her mother's neck and, displaying her latest trick, pressed her warm puffy mouth to the cheek in a sloppy kiss.

'Clever girl,' Elizabeth tousled her hair, and then kissed her back. 'Come say hello.'

'Nannie, Nannie, Nannie,' the child chanted, and the responding cracked voice came back from the dining room.

'Where's my girl? Where's my Kate girl?'

Elizabeth carried her out and placed her into the highchair, handing her a rusk.

'She gets cuter by the day,' declared Louise, winning instant approval.

Elizabeth nodded.

'I have a present from London for you darling,' Louise said, producing a soft doll. 'My Lottie thought you might like it.'

Kate narrowed her eyes and looked into the face of the doll, peered around it at Annie who nodded encouragingly, then looked at her mother, 'Mine?' Kate said clearly.

'She said mine, she said mine,' Annie was hopping up and down on the lounge, twisted hands describing windmills in the air. 'I've been teaching her that word. Look I taught her to say mine.'

They were all laughing and Elizabeth took the doll from Louise and put it in Annie's crumb-coated hands. Suddenly the doll was up against the little girl's face receiving a loud kiss. 'Mine,' she said again more confidently.

'I think she likes it,' said Louise, 'I must tell Lottie.'

Elizabeth wrote to Lottie and sent a photo of Kate and her new dolly. A postcard came back saying *Wish You Were Here – well not really – glad you're with my grandma. Love Lottie.*

The family were always saying Annie seemed younger, happier and more energetic. Annie's youngest daughter, Jean, herself a grandmother, confided one day, 'The difference in Mum is just phenomenal. She has so much more interest in life now. We can't thank you enough, Liz. None of us could have done better.' Elizabeth flushed and started to reply that she owed Annie much more, but Jean stopped her, 'That's what life's all about, dear, helping one another.'

Jean encouraged her to go to a playgroup at their church. Through painting and playdough and playtime, she slowly formed relationships with other young mums. Lee, Jean's daughter, took her two littlies along and the two young women became great friends, often visiting each other and taking the children out to the park together. Annie would come along to playgroup when she was up to it and discovered she loved being back at church events. They attended Sunday services as often as possible, but she missed the other gatherings. 'You know, I used to love coming to all the kids' stuff and the ladies' meetings. I'd like a dollar for every dozen scones

I cooked over the years. Even a cent and I'd be a millionaire. This is where I was christened, and married, and brought my kids. I remember like yesterday the service we had at the end of the Great War for my Gus and the other blokes that were all buried overseas. It helped a bit – thinking of them Gone Home but sort of still with us. We got up the money from the town and had a board made with their names on it so they wouldn't be forgotten.'

Elizabeth held her.

'I'm okay.' Annie shone her beautiful crepe paper smile. 'It was all such a long time ago. I think we all wondered what God was thinking when He let so many of our men die over there. But then I found peace here and accepted His plan for my life. And I know when I go to heaven, Gus'll be waiting there for me. We both believed, see. I'll be going home to him.'

Tears ran down Elizabeth's cheeks, but Annie was having none of it. 'Come on, lots to be done, get out that playdough,' she'd say, crinkling her nose in disgust at the stuff, 'let's give these kids something to do before they put a ball through the stained-glass window. Again.'

Chapter 8

Elizabeth was beginning to be acknowledged as a restorer of old houses. It began with advice on decorating and soon escalated in full-blown renewals. Annie talked non-stop about the great job Elizabeth had done on her old house and invited people to come and see. She would introduce Elizabeth as the miracle-worker, much to her protégé's chagrin. The young woman learnt the art of fitting needs to budgets, using her mother's maiden name for any suppliers so there was no chance of being recognised. Annie's knowledge of local tradesmen was invaluable and she loved contributing to local employment. Kate often came along and Annie insisted on inspecting the jobs before and after so she could skite some more. Steadily the threads of life were drawing together.

Lottie blew into town on the spring breeze. Elizabeth had occasionally written to her overseas, but this was the first time they had been together. Telling everybody she'd come for a week's holiday with her favourite grandma, Lottie sang funny songs for Kate and doubled everyone up with her outrageous stories about the hotel world. After Annie had gone to bed one evening, she became suddenly serious and asked what had happened two years earlier. Elizabeth couldn't bring herself to tell everything, and never mentioned Martin's name, so Lottie looked angry at the end. 'You know, not long after you left, Warren Nichols rang and asked if I knew where you were?'

Elizabeth's stomach flipped over and tied itself into a knot. She shook her head in silent disbelief.

'I never knew how he got my name and I pleaded ignorance very innocently. You'd have been proud. And you didn't put him in hospital you know, it was some outraged husband.

Anyway, he's gone now. Just after Christmas he left the state with his newest secretary. I think his wife was relieved to see the back of him. Tracey's set up on her own out in the Western suburbs. The old company think she's small fry, but she's doing very well in her own way.'

Elizabeth's nausea subsided and they talked more about Tracey. As she was saying goodbye Lottie said, 'You know, I think Tracey would be glad to have you back if you ever wanted to. This,' she waved her hand around the room, 'is wonderful. Authentic, but not overpowering. And it's so homey and comfortable. You have so much talent. It's a waste not to use it. Think it over,' she urged.

'I'm happy here. In fact, I've never known happiness like this before.'

'You know Granny is still frail, even if she is the life of the party.' Lottie put her arms around her friend to take the sting out her ominous words.

Meanwhile, Kate grew and talked more and more. Annie delighted in singing nursery rhymes and loved Kate's version of them. She still called the child, 'My lovely Kate,' and was delighted now with Kate's answer 'My lubbly Nannie.' Annie was fascinated by Kate's toddler talk and even more so because it brought back happy memories of her own children and grandchildren. Kate was equally fascinated by Annie's ageless stories and rhymes. They were the happiest of families. John still came visiting and had lately been bringing his Janet. His eyes shone with a light he had never had for Elizabeth and she was pleased she had not imagined anything else in the relationship. Janet was a lovely girl, all agreed, and just right for John.

Christmas was glorious in the old house that year. With Kate toddling around and chattering about the tree and the *decidations*. Kate loved her dinky that Santa brought. Christmas day was celebrated first at church singing 'Joy to the World' – a fitting start. Then on to Jean's house with the whole family. Cold turkey, ham and luscious salads, followed by hot Christmas pudding with all the trimmings. Throughout the hot summer afternoon, people dozed in the house, sleeping off the feast while the children played on the wide verandas with their Christmas toys. Reluctantly, Kate went home for a much-needed nap in the late afternoon. Throughout the evening, various people called to see Annie and wish her a Merry Christmas, share some fruit cake and admire the house. Elizabeth had never had such a happy, joyous, love-filled Christmas.

Harvest, the following year, brought Annie a terrible shock. Jean's youngest daughter, Ellen was found dead from a stroke. She was cold in her bed when her husband brought in the header from a night harvest. Annie was inconsolable. 'Why Ellen?' she cried. 'Three small children and no mother – how will they cope? Why not me? Look at me, old and useless and I can't even look after them.'

'You are not useless,' Elizabeth assured her. 'Look what you've done for me. I'm not your blood, but if Kate and I hadn't had you, where would we be?' Annie just shook her head and clung, sobbing.

Kate stayed with a friend from playgroup while Elizabeth took Annie to the funeral. Jean wanted her mother to stay at home, so pale and thin and bent Annie had become. But the old woman would have none of it. It was her place, she insisted, the church where she welcomed and farewelled her loved ones. As they were leaving the church, Lee beckoned. From the side chapel a cry rang out. Annie had lost her footing, slipped on a small step and pitched face forward. She lay on the floor moaning in pain. 'No, no, no,' Jean was crying. The ambulance was summoned. Elizabeth sat beside Annie to the hospital, gripping her hand which was stiff with agony. At the hospital they Xrayed the joint and explained Annie had broken her hip. She would have to be hospitalised until it healed and her bones were very fragile.

All through the winter that year and on into spring Annie's old bones refused to heal. She lay in her bed, trying to be bright, bringing tears to all her loved-ones' eyes. As summer turned on its clear blue sky, it became apparent that Annie was going home, sliding towards heaven. Her family came to see her regularly. Jean prayed with her, Lee told her playgroup stories, John brought Janet to say they were engaged, and Lottie sent cards from exotic places twice a week. The end was inevitable. Jean described Annie as having one foot in paradise and Elizabeth sorrowfully agreed.

And Annie knew. 'This is the finish of me,' she confided to Elizabeth one warm day, the sun blessing her bed in benediction, dust motes dancing in its beams.

'No, no Annie,' Elizabeth said, 'You still have lots of life in you yet.'

'It's okay, you know,' her voice was crackling in and out, 'I'm happy to go to Jesus. See Gus again – and Ellen.' Her eyes were half closed. 'One more thing,' she murmured drowsily, 'You need to tell Kate's dad about her.' Her eyelids fluttered onto her cheeks, oblivion pulling her under again.

And they were her final words to her young companion.

Kate and Elizabeth kissed her goodbye, for the last time. Barely breathing, Annie seemed hardly conscious but smiled briefly when Kate wrapped her little arms around her crinkled neck and kissed her parchment cheek. No more worries for her – just peace. What did she dream of in those slow, closing days, when she flitted in and out of consciousness?

The world had altered vastly before her eyes. She'd seen it all: droughts, fires, floods, wars; the coming of gas, electricity, radios, cars, movies, inside bathrooms, flushing toilets, dishwashers and television - that left her flabbergasted. What was eternal, was love – of her family, of her friends and of her God. Annie died quietly, surrounded by them all – including Elizabeth.

There was no surprise at her passing, but there was still shock. The family were very kind but now, with Annie gone, it was time for Elizabeth to strike out on her own. When the will was read, Annie had left her a sum of money. This, together with the balance of Elizabeth's mother's estate, and recent earnings provided some once longed-for security. Happily, John was buying the old house from the estate. He and Janet had always loved it – and the restoration. Annie's place would be in safe hands. Elizabeth packed her belongings once more, this time with lots of little clothes and teddy bears and toys.

Lottie, of course, had flown in for the funeral and urged contact with Tracey. Elizabeth rang her old boss and made arrangements to meet under the clock at Central station. Tracey would organise somewhere to stay until they were settled, and an interview for a job with her firm.

After long and hard deliberations, Elizabeth finally took off the old wedding ring and gave it to Lee before leaving. 'It's really yours. Annie gave it to me to stop gossip.'

Lee knew. 'Country towns are the worst,' she screwed her mouth, 'too much time on their hands. They love to talk. I'm glad you were able to wear it while you were here. After all,' she hugged Elizabeth, 'you are one of the family.'

The Websters gave mother and daughter a royal send-off, extracting a promise to come back and visit them any time, and to stay in touch no matter what. *Don't be a stranger,* was their favourite expression, and Elizabeth reflected she had been a stranger in the world for most of her life but no longer felt like one. Thanks to Annie.

Chapter 9

Kate loved the train trip. Bouncing up and down on the seat through the farmland, pointing out all the *aminals*. Face pressed against the window, through the mountains spotting brightly coloured mountain Rosellas and King parrots cavorting through the forest. Snuggled up against her mummy commenting on everchanging suburbs and awestruck by the city, she kept fellow passengers highly amused.

Shyness – maybe tiredness – overcame her when they met Tracey at Central Station and she buried her face in her mother's skirt. 'Never mind,' said Tracey, 'she'll get used to me. And

I'm giving you an interview on the way.' They climbed into her car. 'Do you have any plans?'

Elizabeth thanked her for her kindness. Kate was almost comatose. All the excitement had dropped out of her and she was glad to nestle into her mother's lap on the back seat. 'Well, I have what we need for a little while, and when I'm settled, I can have the rest sent on. I thought I'd stay at a motel near you until we can find a flat.'

'Right, off to the motel then.' Tracey proceeded to drive out along the long road to Campbelltown, where she now lived. They pulled up outside a group of town houses. Tracey opened the door and ushered in her guests. Elizabeth carried a sleeping Kate and protested vigorously in a whisper so as not to wake her up.

Tracey refused to take no for an answer. 'Welcome to my Home Motel. I thought you might like to stay with me until you're settled.' She had set up her spare room so they could share it. Kate opened her eyes as she was laid down and was enchanted with her little bed, as she called the cot without its sides that Tracey had borrowed. The room was filled with the warm golden light of late afternoon, bouncing off the daffodil yellow bedspread and curtains. They put Kate's toys on her bed and showed her the view from the window across the countryside dotted with town houses and trees.

'Very restful,' Elizabeth told Tracey, as they toured the house.

'Yes, it's new but I like it fine. Nice neighbours and I can look out of every window and have a view.'

'Tracey, I can't thank you enough.'

'Don't mention it.' She smiled and handed over a glass of sherry. 'The truth is, I've always felt a bit responsible for what happened to you.'

Elizabeth shook her head as they perched on high stools at the breakfast bar.

'You were so young and vulnerable and what with losing your mother – well – after you'd gone, I felt I should have protected you more. I should have spoken out about Warren – the worm – and there were other situations I shouldn't have put you in.'

'We're all responsible for ourselves in the long run.' Elizabeth sounded very grown-up and independent. Was she channelling Annie? All that common sense training had created a sensible Liz voice.

Tracey nodded thoughtfully and then went on, 'I found out after you left that Warren told you he'd got you that job. That just wasn't true, Liz. We all had to give our opinions on the applicants. You're a very talented girl, you know. You won that job on your own merit. So Warren approved of you – so what? – so did I – and several others.' She sipped the sherry slowly and gazed at her friend. 'And I would count myself very fortunate if you agree to join my firm. It's not charity, you know.' With those simple words, Tracey restored any last doubts Elizabeth had about her move. 'Anyway,' she continued, 'what had you intended to do? You must have some ideas.'

'I've been restoring houses. Did you know that?'

Tracey nodded gravely and it made Elizabeth wonder what Lottie had said.

'I'd like to do more of that. Do you get much work in that line?'

'A bit.' Tracey looked thoughtful. 'Probably more with you on board. We can offer that as a speciality. What do you need to work?'

'I guess the first thing I need is a small car. I don't suppose you run to a company car, do you?'

Tracey's eyebrows nearly hit her fringe.

'No that's not fair. Forget I said that.'

This time Tracey laughed. 'No doubt about you, you know how to bargain.'

A chuckle rose up from deep in Elizabeth's belly but she carried on regardless, 'Then I must find somewhere to live and a day nursery for Kate. When that's done, I can send for the rest of my gear and start working.' It seemed straightforward and easy, summed up like that. Where did that plan come from? *Thanks God,* she found herself thinking. There was Annie again.

Kate wandered down the stairs and they settled her on the lounge in front of the TV.

Tracey smiled. 'Would you like to hear my plans? Well, suggestions, really.' This sounded hopeful. 'Firstly, your wage will include a car allowance, so we can organise a car fairly rapidly. Secondly, as you can see from this place, I sometimes use my home to demonstrate my styles. I like to bring uncertain clients here so they can see I won't turn their homes into horror chambers. Lately, I've had several enquiries from people with small children. One visitor pointed out she wouldn't like to see her little monster let loose in here.'

That would be the Delft figurines on low tables – and the silk curtains.

'Well, now you mention it, I could just raise this a little.' Elizabeth picked up the porcelain ladies and put them safely out of Kate's reach. She was a good girl, but she did love pretty things.

Kate looked up appreciatively at it. 'Pretty lady,' she murmured and then returned to her Sesame Street, 'Bert's lost his nose.'

'How does he smell?' her mother asked, knowing the answer.

'Terrible.' They sniggered together.

Elizabeth left her to the TV and returned to the kitchen.

'I didn't mean Kate, you know. She looks well trained,' Tracey said reassuringly.

'Yes, she's been brought up to look not touch. Annie lived with her antiques and believed in enjoying the house even after it was restored. But sometimes curiosity gets the better of her. She's gentle, but accidents happen.'

'The town house next door is going on the market. I'll be sorry to see the couple go, they've been good neighbours. They've agreed to give me a first option on the place. I want to redecorate it and rent it out to a family with a youngster. Make it suitably practical and beautiful as well. Seems to me you might be just right for it. It's virtually the same floor plan as this, so Kate would have her own room.' Elizabeth was trying to protest but her boss was unstoppable. 'It would be bought and maintained by the firm. Of course, your rent would take into consideration that it would be needed as a show place from time to time.'

'Tracey, that sounds perfect. But please don't do it just for me.' Elizabeth's eyes filled with tears and she touched her friend's arm. Every nerve in her body tingled then relaxed. They would have a home again.

Tracey shook her head. 'I'd already decided to buy the place before I heard from you. And I've asked around about preschools and found a couple that look good. There's one not too far away from the office. With flexible working hours so you can work at home as well, it would be eminently suitable.'

'I just can't thank you enough for everything.'

Tracey shook her head. 'You always gave it one hundred percent and were so talented. I couldn't think of anyone I'd rather work beside.'

They agreed to sleep on it and Elizabeth would reply in the morning.

What does joy feel like? Sunset setting clouds aflame. Birdsong at dusk. The ghost of sherry on the tongue. Kind words of a friend. A warm hug before bed. And sunlight's scent in fresh sheets. So, of course, the answer was YES. This was the perfect situation, a job worth doing, with a secure position and a much-loved boss. Annie would have approved. Her common-sense approach to life had provided a new inner voice of wisdom. Taking things at face value, and being grateful for small mercies, as she said, had taught a less judgemental perception of the world. It had also inspired a sensible inner conversation that steadied Elizabeth and made her feel of value.

Chapter 10

Kate, Tracey and Elizabeth rubbed along very well. As her mother settled into the job, Kate lost her shyness with Tracey. They began to enjoy books and jokes and TV shows together. The sale of the unit next door progressed fairly rapidly and, while it was going through, they developed designs for the decoration. Elizabeth was given the final say.

'After all you know what suits a child, and you have to live in it,' Tracey reassured her. During the time, she bought a small car and settled Kate into the Pre-School. Kate loved going along, seeing it as an extension of the playgroup she had enjoyed in Cowra. She was confident to say goodbye on the first day and the following day proudly said she was a big girl and could take herself.

'Kate's fine,' said Mrs Phillips, the lady in charge. 'She's such a loveable little thing. She'll make a good mum one day, the way she fusses over those dollies.' Kate talked endlessly about Christopher, the little boy who played mummies and daddies with her. Apparently, they couldn't quite decide who'd be the mummy and push the pram until Mrs. Phillips suggested that both mummies and daddies pushed prams, so they could take turns. Tracey and Elizabeth had a quiet laugh over that. Mrs. Phillips also said the pair loved to pretend it was raining so they could put on their yellow raincoats, hats and boots and hop around in imaginary puddles. Which was better, she stated with raised eyebrows, than the children who liked to pretend they were at the beach and kept stripping off all their clothes. Kate enjoyed it all so much she sometimes resisted coming home. Stormy days were easy because, once the yellow ensemble was whipped out, she was pulling it on, ready to run out in the rain. She had never seen storms like this before.

Clapping her hands and bouncing on the spot like a seal pup, she could hardly be wrestled into the bright yellow coat.

They moved into the new place just in time to put up a Christmas tree. Tracey admitted she had never been so excited about the festive season since she was a child. She was having the time of her life buying a tree and decorating it with Kate, whose favourite were the angels – and she wanted them all over – not just on the top. Tracey came home with a beautiful music box angel that played 'Silent Night' and Kate was entranced. Each night they had to play it before Kate went to bed.

Lottie was back in Sydney for the holiday season. She didn't have time to return to Cowra because of work so Elizabeth invited her for Christmas Day. Lee sent a lovely newsy card and Lottie shared the family gossip. Elizabeth struggled to hold back the tears. 'I know she had a long life, Lottie, but I miss Annie dreadfully.'

Lottie held her friend. 'She'd be proud of you two here. She wanted you to have a future.' Elizabeth knew the truth. Annie had also wanted her to get in touch with Martin and tell him about Kate. But that was never going to happen.

They spent a lovely day together talking about family and work with regular doses of 'Silent Night'. Tracey came over in the evening and the four made a very merry time.

The New Year rolled around once more, and life and business continued. Elizabeth managed to pick up some restorations.

Tracey adored Kate who, in turn, idolised her. 'You know Liz,' Tracey remarked one evening, 'I might want my career badly, but I also love children. Well, I particularly love Kate. And I have decided that one of my aims for the business should be thinking about the whole family.'

Elizabeth sometimes took Kate with her to client's homes so they could discuss their needs. The presence of the decorator's child instilled confidence that she could come up with a suitable new plan for their houses and children. Kate kept occupied with her little backpack full of colouring pencils, books and puzzles.

Summer's heat ebbed into autumn's cool nights. At the beginning of winter Kate celebrated her fourth birthday. They invited a few of her friends from preschool, including the charming Christopher who stated quite firmly as he gazed at Kate's new dolly, 'You know I'm the daddy now.' The adults laughed. What could they say? Elizabeth made fairy bread, fairy cakes and angel food cake. And had to assure Kate that, contrary to Aunty Tracey's comment, none were made from either real fairies or former angels.

The cooler weather came and one crisp July day Tracey called her over to her place to discuss a new assignment.

'Sit down, Liz. I have a favour to ask of you.' Tracey's face was tinged with red and she looked slightly guilty. She rushed on. 'I had a call from an old friend of yours today, Martin Fielding. He'd heard you were back working with me and he'd like you to decorate a new addition to his house. I believe you did the original designs?'

You know I damn-well did, Elizabeth thought, her brain freezing to ice like frost in the dawn.

However, she held her tongue and just nodded, deadpan.

'I would have done it myself, dear, but he especially asked for you, it's only a small job and you *did* do the rest of the house.'

Sunlight poured in through the closed windows and pooled around the chair. Elizabeth felt disembodied, away somewhere in a dark bedroom gazing at sleeping Martin, the scent of the new wood in her nostrils, the taste of love on her mouth. She'd never actually told anybody the name of Kate's father. Her head shook slowly from side to side of its own volition. There was a monologue going on in her brain. *What can he do to you now? You're an adult not that naïve kid. Should be a quick job. Remain professional.* It seemed reasonable.

'Are you okay?' asked Tracey.

'Fine, just fine.'

Tracey nodded, shuffling her pages. The blush was ebbing from her cheeks, leaving them pale. 'Good then. I've made an appointment for you to visit his house about 8pm Friday evening. He's very busy at work at present and can't make it through the daytime.'

She nodded encouragingly, and, although Elizabeth's gut was clenched into a hard ball, she bared her teeth in a semblance of a smile.

'I'll come in and put Kate to bed for you. How about we have an early dinner together first?'

As if she'd be able to eat, the voice inside said. Tracey had provided an income, a place to live and unending love and attention. She *could* not refuse this request.

That Friday Elizabeth laboured at her job, ignoring what was to come. The three enjoyed their evening meal - on the surface. Tracey and Kate certainly did, while Elizabeth chased hers around the plate and laughed in a brittle fashion at anything remotely funny. Tracey never commented, reserving her attention for her talkative little mate.

Wearing her most austere business suit, Elizabeth packed the car in professional efficiency and drove obligingly to meet her fate.

The house had changed. Trees around it had shot up and out over the four years and it seemed both more substantial and more in the bush. She sat in the car staring at the red front door, summoning the courage to approach. That sensible inside voice was working overtime. Self-talk is such a bonus, it boosts the confidence, comforts the soul and sends ordinary mortals in where angels fear to tread – so Annie had said. So, Elizabeth climbed out, picked up her bag, shut the car door with a bang, made her feet walk one after the other down the path, raised her right index finger and pressed the bell button. An Avon-calling chime rang through the house accompanied by the barking of a dog somewhere in the depths. A light came on in the hallway, shining through the panes either side of the front door. The door was flung open and Martin stood there in the hallway, a brindle collie at his side.

Chapter 11

Instantly Elizabeth knew it was wrong. The feeling exploded through her whole being like a Catherine wheel on fireworks night. She was struggling to control her breathing, nearly hyperventilating. If young Martin had been charming and handsome, mature Martin was overwhelming. There was his familiar wood-chip scent. The memory of the taste of his kiss. His welcoming voice reverberated through her ribcage, making her heart pound like a bunch of four-year-olds on red cordial. The case in her hand felt like a dead weight on her conscience. *Pull yourself together,* sensible Liz was shouting she grabbed what words she could find and complimented him on his house, ignoring the fact that most of it was her own design.

He led her through to the lounge and the dog preceded them, flopping down in front of the fireplace. 'Take a seat Liz,' he said, with his heart-melting smile. 'Can I offer you a drink – or tea or coffee?'

Easy question to answer. Just swallow. 'No thanks, I've just had dinner.'

'You're looking fine,' that devastating smile again as he sat opposite. 'Quite the business woman.'

She summoned a stiff grimace and nodded.

'Tracey was lucky to get you back from that other decorating firm.'

Was that a statement or a question? *So, that's what Tracey said about her absence.* Later, lying in bed without sleep endlessly examining every word, it dawned on her that Tracey had tried to offer protection. For the moment, she was concentrating hard on the keeping up with the conversation.

'The house is looking good,' she said, gazing around. 'It's certainly kept its style. It looks like its liveable.'

'Certainly is,' said Martin. 'You did a great job on it. I love living here. And it suits me perfectly. Would you like to see the rest of the house and the new additions?'

She rose, leaving behind her bag, and he guided her out through the other rooms once filled from her creative little heart. As they passed his bedroom, her stomach hit rock bottom and bounced up again into her throat. One glance, and she was hurrying along towards the kitchen and the new extensions.

The house was now U-shaped, with a new wing added on one side forming a courtyard with a new swimming pool in the middle. Martin led the way to the pool area first, the dog padding after them, and switched on the lighting. Beautifully landscaped, it backed into the bushland and had a safety fence all around.

'I wanted to feel like I was in a forest pool,' he explained as they hung over the fence watching the lights dappling on the water. 'This,' he touched the fence, 'is to keep out my nephews. My sister Julie moved out to the country a couple of years ago and likes to come visiting. Actually, that's why I put on the extension. It has a couple of extra bedrooms, a bathroom and a rumpus room. I enjoy their visits. … and, I confess, the rumpus room is for my electric train set, not that I have much time to play with it.' He smiled ruefully, endearingly, whispered her heart, dangerously, corrected that inner voice.

'It's lovely,' she sighed and then snapped back to reality. *Come on business Liz,* her brain was chiding, get on with it. 'Let's have a look at the extension and make some plans.' They walked back into the new wing which was completely empty, its unpainted walls begging to be splashed with colour. She pulled out her tape, notebook and pen and measured walls and floors. 'I have some sample books in my car, I'll just get them.' She began to rise.

Martin stood in her way and put his hand out, 'Give me the car keys and I'll fetch them. I feel a bit useless just standing here. I'll put the dog to bed as I go. You go and sit in the lounge and get on with your plans.'

Seemed sensible, that voice said. Although, her foolish heart would have had her jumping off a cliff if he asked.

As she sketched away, Martin came back into the lounge his arms filled with samples and catalogues. They discussed the uses of the rooms, what might be suitable for his future guests and how it could be made flow and also detach from the rest of the house. They poured over books and samples, choosing options along the way. Elizabeth suddenly looked at her watch and realised it was eleven o'clock. Panic gripped and she began packing up. 'I must go.'

'Let's have a coffee first before you go back out into the cold. Then I'll carry all this stuff out for you,' suggested Martin. 'I put the coffee percolator on a little while ago.'

He left the room as she put the last of the samples into neat piles, and returned with two steaming mugs. Sitting down on an ottoman opposite her, he pulled a photo out of his pocket. It was Kate at her birthday party with four blazing candles on the cake and Elizabeth helping her blow them out. It had been collected from the chemist today – and been left on the front passenger seat. 'She's a beautiful child,' he said. 'And she looks just like you.'

Elizabeth had to put the mug down quickly. She was choking on the hot drink, which was burning her sinuses and streaming out her nose.

He handed over a box of tissues and waited, and waited. Finally, he spoke. 'She also looks like me. Or, to be more correct, her cousins.' He took a photo of his three nephews off the mantle-shelf and held it up. Same eyes.

Elizabeth's mouth opened but the anticipated lies dried on her lips. She suddenly remembered Annie's last words. He did deserve to know. Her head bobbed up and down like the darkened trees outside bowing to the night wind. He rose from his seat, put down his coffee and walked over to the glass doors, staring out into the darkness, the stars bright outside haloing his reflection in the glass. It felt like a lifetime passed – caught in still life.

An enormous sigh came forth from the bottom of her diaphragm, voiding her whole body and breaking the inertia.

At once Martin turned from the window and Elizabeth realised that the droplets rolling down the glass she had taken for condensation on the inside of the glass were tears on his cheeks. 'Why didn't you tell me?'

Sadness was warring with anger.

'Well?' He wasn't giving up easily.

'What would you have done? What would your family have said? When would you have had time for a child?' The long-held dam was broken, unleashing from the depths of her being. 'Just because you're the biological father, you don't have to feel responsible for her. We get along just fine.' She rose from the chair, gathering what she could. 'Thanks for the coffee. I'll have the final drawings to you as soon as possible and the job will be costed and completed in good time.' She strode out to the front door and, as she flung it open, realised he still had her car keys.

'Running away again, are you?' he growled. 'Don't you ever finish anything?' He grabbed her by the wrist, led her back into the lounge room and pushed her unceremoniously down onto the sofa. 'Now,' he barked, 'we're going to discuss this in an adult fashion.'

Elizabeth was feeling anything but adult. She wanted to scream and shout and throw things about like some of Mrs. Phillip's preschoolers. Business Liz had vanished. She was in deep panic. Words coagulated in her mouth.

'Let me tell you how I felt when you left me.' His deep voice pierced her thoughts.

Elizabeth opened her mouth to speak, but the red grasp of his rage stopped her dead.

'There you were running away from me, burning the miles between us, while I laboured on trying to get as much done as I could so I could have time to spend with you, blissfully unaware that you were long gone.' A shuddering sigh racked his long body. 'I rang Tracey and got the frozen treatment from her. She said you were unavailable. Unavailable – that's one word for it. They made me feel like a lecher. I had to fight with the company to get your designs completed here.' He swept his long hand around and then collapsed back onto the ottoman in front of her, his head bent into his hands. Eventually he looked up and said more quietly, 'People talk, you know, they sort out their relationships. What did I say to make you go?' His voice cracked.

Tears welled in her eyes, spilled down the sides of her nose and ran into her mouth. Memory rose unbidden like a snake up a pole.

'How much you liked being young with the freedom to do what you wanted.'

His eyebrows rose. 'Did I say that? Well, I guess I thought we both were. Was that why you didn't tell me about … her?' He brandished the photo.

She wiped her cheeks with the heel of her hand and gulped. 'No man will ever say he had to marry me. I managed – we manage – fine.'

His head was slowly revolving from side to side, but his red-hot anger seemed to have drained like lava into the sea.

Elizabeth was dog tired. Fight or flight adrenaline had made her do both. Too exhausted to stand, too addled to stand up for herself, too drained to stand up to him. Wordless inertia was all that remained. There could be no winner in this situation.

'You look spent,' he eventually said. 'Let me drive you home.' He waved away her protests. 'You can collect your car tomorrow. I'll come and pick you up. I don't want you driving in this state.' And, like his obedient collie, she followed him out the red door to his car. Wedged somewhere between rebellion at his high handedness and relief at his caring, her common-sense voice was mute.

An icy wind had blown up outside and the treetops were roaring as they silently drove through the brittle starlit night. Elizabeth had an eerie sense that she was alone, passing through another dimension, out into an unknown world with strange boundaries. It was a shock when they stopped outside her home. Martin climbed out, came around and opened the passenger door. Reality suddenly caught up as he gripped her forearm and the tingle shot through her nervous system.

'What time in the morning?' he asked quietly.

'Perhaps Tracey can bring me out.'

His eyes narrowed. 'Or I can. What time?'

Oddly she thought about the vacuuming and scrubbing the bathroom and almost laughed. She did like a Saturday morning clean. Sensible Liz had finally shown up. 'Around eleven?' Business Liz was back in business. What would she do with Kate? She glanced up at the fairy decal on the bedroom window, wishing for magic dust.

'Okay.' He was nodding, 'I'll come over and get you at eleven.'

Not the sort of answer she was looking for but it seemed non-negotiable – and reasonable – said in that calm tone. She nodded and went to turn away when his hand moved up to her shoulder.

'Listen, Liz,' he whispered, 'I promise I won't say anything to her. Just call me Marty, a friend from work.'

Her head bounced up and down and he let her go, the warm imprint of his hand on her shoulder casting a blast of shooting sparks from torso to toes. Playing with matches and a girl could get well and truly burned. It would take a miracle to put out this fire.

So they parted. Martin speeding back to his house and Elizabeth attempting to patch together her fractured life.

As she slipped through the door, Tracey was working at the dining room table. She looked up and smiled. 'How did it go?' She began packing up her papers and gathering other belongings.

'Good.' What a lie, sensible Liz screamed. *Good? Good? Catastrophic more like.* 'How was Kate?' she said, struggling thoughts through brain chaos.

'Great – as always. I did enjoy her new book. *The Pokey Little Puppy.*' She smiled. 'She wants a dog now.'

'She wants lots of things,' came out of her mouth and Elizabeth wondered who *she* was, daughter or mother.

'I'll be off then,' Tracey scooted out the door.

Elizabeth should have asked if Tracey could drive her to Martin's the next day. She should have told her that Martin knew about Kate. She should have put her hands around her boss's neck and squeezed and squeezed. Up the stairs she trudged, and took a quick look at her darling, curled up and coverless. Pulling up her fairy quilt, she kissed the coppery head. Kate murmured something incoherent and then plugged her thumb back into her cherub mouth. Retreating into the dark bedroom, Elizabeth was too mind-blasted to do any more than flop on the bed like a dying fish.

Chapter 12

That night she dreamt of Annie. For two fraught hours she had told herself she must sleep, but her brain hopped around like a four-year-old in rainboots. It was raining in her brain but her stubborn heart refused to release the deluge. Neither could she relax enough to tip over the edge into oblivion. She began to pray, as she had heard Annie do from the next room when the old lady's pain drove sleep away. Obviously, oblivion obliged, because she found herself sitting under the orange tree with Annie. They were laughing together so hard that Elizabeth was doubled up and Annie was holding onto her belly with one hand to stop having what she called *a bladder incident.* Perched in her white cane chair under the bee rich blossom, she gripped Elizabeth's hand tight in her other gnarled twisted fingers. Tears were pouring down – happy tears – and Elizabeth was rocking back and forth. Annie pulled her towards her into her arms, strong with years of kneading, and they shook together.

'Wake up, Mummy, wake up.' And it was Kate's starfish hand shaking her shoulder. She was standing by the bed in her flannelette angel jammies. 'Why are you crying?'

'It's so funny,' Elizabeth managed to spit out eventually.

'Then why is your face wet?' Kate's eyes and lips were screwed up with puzzlement.

Elizabeth swayed in the bed, laughing, with tears coursing down her cheeks, 'Well,' she gasped, 'it's just that…' And suddenly, and at once, it left her. She had no idea. The dream had flown, and the joke was over. That was the best laugh she'd had for months, but the joke had vanished like morning mist.

Kate looked at her expectantly.

'I've no idea.' Elizabeth admitted.

'Well,' said her daughter, disgusted now. 'It's past brekkie time and I'm hungry.'

They hurried through the housework. Kate loved to dust and tidy up. Cleaning and scrubbing and putting away was a welcome distraction. Well nearly. Elizabeth toyed with the idea of asking Tracey to take Kate while she collected the car, but Tracey was unreachable. *Hmm*, Elizabeth thought, in unison with the vacuum cleaner, *suspicious*. By ten thirty they were all done.

'Can we go to the park?' asked Kate

'Maybe later.' Suddenly, sensible Liz was in charge. 'I left my car at a work friend's place last night and he's coming over to drive me back to pick it up. After that we could go to the park.' Getting a grip. 'And do some food shopping.' All perfectly normal here, nothing to be worried about.

Kate's eyes danced. 'Can we buy cocoa pops for breakfast?'

'You know better than that. It's not holidays.'

The girl pouted slightly then her face lit up, 'What about another golden book?'

'If you're a good girl.' Negotiation was a wonderful thing, but she was always a good girl really. Elizabeth made both a cup of tea – Kate's mostly milk. They settled down to wait as the little girl recited *The Pokey Little Puppy*.

'What's his name?' she asked at the end of page three.

'Isn't the dog's name in the book?'

'What book?' she screwed up her nose.

Elizabeth pointed at the one she was holding.

'Your friend's name - not the book, Silly,' she laughed.

'I thought you meant the puppy,' Elizabeth answered, really buying time.

Kate's copper curls shook with her laughter.

Might as well get it over. 'His name is Martin Fielding. You can call him Mr. Fielding.'

Kate flipped the page absently, intoning, 'That pokey little puppy, that pokey little puppy.' Lulling her mother into a trance.

Bing, Bong. It was exactly eleven when the doorbell chimed and Elizabeth nearly went through the carefully painted ceiling. She leapt out of the chair and rushed to the front door. She should be over this reddening that started at her waist, slowly made its way over her torso, up her neck, flooding her cheeks and ending in the roots of her hair. But no. She could feel the tide rising. Kate's footsteps came to a sudden halt behind her.

'Hello,' she chirped as her mother was clinging to the door for balance, 'I'm Kate.'

He bent down and took her hand, 'Hello, I'm Martin.'

Dear God, those eyes smiling at each other.

'Nice to meet you Kate,' he rumbled

'Me too,' said Kate, 'do you like puppies?'

He nodded sagely, 'Sure do. And I like dogs too.'

Where was her customary shyness? This instant connection had blown it all away. Kate pulled him into the lounge room, pushed him onto the lounge, climbed up beside him and thrust her book into his hands. 'Can you please read this to me,' she wheedled.

Elizabeth sat in the lounge chair staring at them. They were totally enthralled with each other. She was lost. All her plans were dust. The tapestry of her life was unravelling. There was no way back from this. If that pokey little puppy was in trouble, it was nothing to the labyrinth yawning at her feet.

When the story was over, Martin looked up. 'I thought I'd take you out to lunch.' He raised his eyebrows in question.

Elizabeth's head was shaking back and forth like a rag doll. 'I can't. I'm not dressed for it. I have Kate. We have to go shopping.'

'Anything else?' he asked

She was trying to make sense of his question.

'That's four excuses. Let me answer them.' There was that heart-warming smile again. 'You can because you look great, I expected that both of you could come and we can go shopping along the way.'

What could she say? *No? She didn't want him in her life. Leave her alone.* With Kate and Martin begging side by side, *no* wasn't possible. And maybe she missed him in her life. And no person on earth really wants to be alone. She caved in.

They had a lovely lunch in a kid-friendly café, then did their shopping, he needed food too. He drove back to his place to pick up the car and *happened* to introduce Kate to his dog, Lady. Prying the girl away from the pooch was difficult, to say the least, until Martin promised she could come again. Or maybe he would bring the dog to their place and they could go to the park together.

Elizabeth eyed him narrowly. So much for the tell-her-I'm-a-business-acquaintance-named-Marty plan, she thought as she put the groceries away after Kate was asleep. Now he's organising play dates with her and the Pokey Little Puppy.

Contrary to Elizabeth's fears, he didn't hound her. The following day, Tracey brought home-made chicken soup and the three shared their usual Sunday lunch. They mostly discussed business and Kate, a never-ending source of intrigue for the boss. Elizabeth caught a furtive, curious glance or two, but ignored them –

deliberately. Business-like Liz was holding the reins today.

She did find a short note in the letterbox on Tuesday afternoon simply saying, *Will ring Friday evening. Hope the plans are going well.*

Whose plans, she thought, and which plans, and plans for anything starting with *wh*. She put her head down, however, and came up with multiple ideas, drawings, and pricings. The sooner it was done, the sooner everything would be over.

On Friday night the phone rang. 'What are you doing tomorrow?' the deep voice asked.

'I'm taking Kate to a kindergarten friend's birthday party in the morning.'

'And after that?'

She couldn't find a right answer. 'A quiet afternoon,' came out of her mouth.

'I thought I might take you both out for lunch again. There's a local place where I can take the dog.'

'It'll be at least one o'clock before we get to you.'

'No problem, I'll book for one thirty or two.'

Surely there had to be some way to get out of this. 'Kate will probably be full of party food.'

'She can play with the dog.'

There was blank silence as she searched for another excuse.

He eventually filled it, 'Why don't you bring your plans over and we can have a look at them over lunch?'

Mmmm. Maybe this would free her from contact with Martin sooner. Maybe she didn't want to be free. There it was, channelling Annie again. He was just so damned charming – and reasonable – and loveable.

Chapter 13

Aren't I lucky,' teased Martin as they walked into the restaurant and were shown out onto the 'pooch patio' with Lady. 'Going out with three lovely ladies for lunch.' Kate did look very pretty in her party dress and Elizabeth may have worn a rainbow flared skirt instead of her habitual jeans. Was that dog smiling at her?

'You can't count, Martin,' piped up Kate, 'there's only Lady – that's your dog. Mum's a woman and I'm a girl.'

'I stand corrected,' said Martin, eyes gleaming with laughter, 'just as well one of us can count.'

Kate stated she was not hungry but they ordered her a bowl of chips and what she lacked in appetite she made up in amusement. Her kindy friend, Christopher had introduced her to jokes and suddenly she had a new audience. Many were her own twists on well-known humour and were hilarious to her and evidently Christopher, but could become wearing. Tracey and Elizabeth had set a limit of five jokes a night.

'Knock, knock,' Martin broke in.

'Say, who's there?' Elizabeth prompted

'Who's there?' she repeated.

'Interrupting cow.'

'Say, interrupting cow who.'

'Interrupting... '

Before she could finish Martin let out a great, 'Moo.'

'Didn't I do it right?' she looked confused.

'You did it right,' her mother assured her, 'Martin was being the interrupting cow and not letting you finish. You know what interrupting means, don't you?'

'Yes.' She nodded confidently. 'That's what I'm not supposed to do when you're talking to somebody, or on the phone, or in the toilet.'

Never work with children or animals, they say. So true. Martin was almost falling off his chair with laughter.

'What. What. Did I tell a good joke?' Kate was bouncing up and down in her seat. Lady sprang up from her sprawling position under the table and barked twice.

'It was a great joke,' said Martin. 'Maybe just between us though.' He eyed Elizabeth cautiously and she nodded. 'Would you like to take Lady down on the lawn and play with her. They have all sorts of toys and she loves to fetch. Is that okay?' He looked at Elizabeth, eyes crinkled from contained mirth, but waiting for agreement.

'Sure,' she said. And off they trotted, down the patio stairs, the girl and the dog, like they'd been doing it all their lives. How proud Annie would have been of this confident young woman.

'She's quite something.' The deep rumble of Martin's voice brought her back to time and place.

Elizabeth turned away from him and gazed out beyond the lawn and over its fringe of bushland. 'Yes, she is.'

'I wish I'd known her for longer. Where did you go Liz?'

She went to speak, to say *just away*, but he rushed on.

'I know you didn't go to another agency in Sydney. I checked them all. And I tried interstate firms as well. I asked everybody that I knew – and nothing. Why did you vanish?' Suddenly he was spent. Run out of questions. His head was shaking sadly, his gaze was on the playmates on the lawn.

His questions were like that nightmare about doors, where one opens to another, and another, and another. She could not – would not answer him. 'Can we look at the plans now?'

He jerked in his chair, shook his head slightly, then turned back, his face composed. 'Sure. Love to.' Resignation drained from him like a deflated balloon. He drew in a deep breath.

The plans were perfect. Of course, they were. Colours were just what he'd imagined. Everything she showed him was greeted with approval. Between flipping through the sketch books, they were glancing at the girl and dog.

Eventually the two playmates dragged themselves back up the stairs to the table. 'She won't catch the ball anymore,' Kate whined and climbed up on her mother's knee. 'And I'm cold.' The best of the sunny winter day was over. Trees' shadows speared along the lawn, and the scent of Eucalyptus wafted in the last rays of sun.

'Lady needs a drink of water,' Martin told her filling one of the dog bowls and watching the dog lap, lap, lap it up. 'And she's probably tired.'

'I think you're tired and need a drink too.' Elizabeth snuggled Kate against her. The girl was rubbing her eyes and yawning widely. 'Would you like a hot chocolate?' Kate's head bobbed up and down.

The waiter came over and Martin ordered hot chocolate with marshmallows, half-filled with cool milk, for her, and cappuccinos for the adults. While they drank them, he paid the bill and then took everyone out into his car. It must have been all of two minutes before both Kate and Lady were fast asleep, sprawled on each other on the back seat.

They took the long way home back to his place. Bundling a waking Kate into Elizabeth's car he simply said, 'I'm sorry Liz.'

Elizabeth shook her head, as she turned on the ignition. Then the words rose as if she had switched on her own truth – and compassion – and regret. 'No, I'm sorry.'

And she drove slowly away, Martin and Lady filling her rear vision mirror, unwavering but diminishing, until she turned onto the main road and they vanished from sight.

The following week was like being stuck in no-man's land. Well, certainly no man named Martin. No calls, no messages, no notes in the letterbox. That's that, over and out. Tracey asked Elizabeth how his project was going and she could truthfully, in a somewhat blasé but certainly businesslike fashion, inform her boss he had approved all the plans and it was up to the costing stage. Once that was done, contractors could be hired. This sounded very efficient on the outside, while her insides were burning.

Kate talked about Martin and Lady, well more about the dog. Christopher had been informed and he was now pressing his parents for a puppy, so his mother said at preschool pick-up.

'All I need's a puppy to clean up after,' moaned his mum, pregnant with her third child under five.

'That's okay,' Kate blithely assured her, 'Christopher can come and play with Lady and me when Martin comes over.'

A sick feeling rose up from Elizabeth's gut. In the nursery school window behind, her face looked like I'd sucked a lemon. Martin may never come again.

Chapter 14

Tracey cornered Elizabeth at Friday lunch time.

'What on earth is wrong with you?' She pushed her employee into the office chair. 'Sit down and tell big sis what the problem is.'

Elizabeth opened her mouth to protest then remembered that, in fact, Tracey had been a big sister. What did little sisters do – or not do? Annie's lessons had paid off. She would let people into her life, against all her mother's training of keeping yourself to yourself. Elizabeth was slowly unravelling, caught in the web of her own tangled principles. 'It's complicated,' she murmured.

'Life's like pick-up-sticks,' Tracey answered, 'It's always complicated.' She waved her hand, as if she could magic all the sticks into line. 'Is it wine o'clock? Would alcohol help unpick this problem?'

Elizabeth shook her head. There wasn't enough wine on earth to sort out this mess.

'Coffee?' Tracey waggled her eyebrows. 'Tea? Bonox? Hot Chocolate?' Her head was in her store cupboard now. 'Cold chocolate? Coke? Lemonade? Screaming soda?'

That brought a laugh. They had hidden the red drink from Kate after one crazy night. Creamng Soda, had more accurately been renamed Screaming Soda.

'I just don't know what to do.' Elizabeth shrugged.

'Martin?'

Elizabeth's head was bobbing up and down of its own volition.

'Earl Grey then, nothing like bergamot to soothe the savage breast. Or is that beast?' Baring her teeth in a grimace and grabbing her favourite teapot from the collection on the top shelf, Tracey put her head back in the fridge. 'And cheese and biscuits.' Tracey bustled about while Elizabeth sank further into the chair, swallowed up by her own doubt.

'So, what's he done?' Tracey slid into the opposite seat.

142

'Nothing.'

Tracey's eyebrows almost hid in her careful hairdo and her shoulders were around her ears.

'Everything.' Elizabeth's hands flew up in despair. Then finally, 'Nothing and everything.'

Tracey took a long sip of tea, her eyes wide, peering over the rim of the cup. 'What worries you most? The nothing or the everything?'

And it poured out, like Earl Grey from the cottage tea-pot, sloshing into the silence and filling all the private spaces. How Martin had discovered Kate, introduced her to his dog, charmed her – and Elizabeth – won them over, asked all those unanswerable questions. And then nothing – silence for nearly a week. How Elizabeth was caught between her new self as an independent, professional woman and her old Martin-infatuated mess. How she had begun to dream of them together, so that both asleep and awake he haunted her. She slugged back the whole cup in one mouthful.

'Oh dear,' said big sister. 'You're a goner.'

'That's not helpful.'

'But true, you'll admit.'

Elizabeth's head inclined in reluctant agreement. 'The real problem is, Kate's talking about him – and his dog – non-stop. This is exactly why I didn't want a man in my life. You cannot depend on them.'

'That's a bit harsh isn't it?'

'I learned that from my mum.' Ancient pain was rising.

'Do you want me to ring him?'

'Definitely not. If he can't care, I don't want him.'

They sat, the silence around like a shroud.

'So, how's his project going?' asked Tracey, bravely, as she refilled their cups.

'Good,' Elizabeth answered firmly. 'Nearly finished. Then I'm done.'

And she was. By Friday afternoon the costings had been couriered to him and there was a very business-like message on his phone asking him to approve them and get them back so the contractors could be organised. 'Done and dusted,' Elizabeth said to Tracey. 'And time for something new.'

'I have several jobs for you,' she said, shuffling through her papers. 'Mostly on Martin's recommendation.'

'Great, now he's put his finger in my work as well.'

'Another day, another dollar.' This was one of Tracey's favourite expressions.

Teeth bared, Elizabeth took the new enquiries out of outstretched hand, put them in her bag and walked out, head high, to pick up Kate from Pre-school.

Chapter 15

Red roses in one hand, a bottle of champagne in the other, an envelope of proposals tucked under his right arm, golden book under his left, Martin managed to knock resoundingly on the front door at eight thirty that night. Kate was already bathed and fed and off to bed and he came in like a willy-willy of enthusiasm and excitement.

Kate jumped out of bed and rushed out to greet him.

'Come my warm little bundle,' he swept her up onto his shoulder, 'let's read a bedtime story together.' And off they went, perched themselves on the lounge and read *The Friendly Book* together. What could Elizabeth say?

'Would you like some coffee?' She came up with when the book was finished and Kate was off to her bedroom to get another.

'I would, thank you.'

'Milk and one sugar?' Politely icy, she hoped.

He nodded and Kate surged back into the room, clambered onto the lounge and nestled into him.

All the things she could have said, sensible Liz was chiding away. Like *what are you doing here,* or *where have you been all week,* or simply *Go Away.* No, no, she had to offer him coffee so he would stay longer. Was that the reason? Who was in control here? Wiping down the kitchen seemed to help. Washing the dishes from dinner, muttering away, wiping up dishes and putting them away, deep in her own head. A whisper from the other room suddenly pierced the brain battle. It had been coming for a while. Martin was sitting on the lounge, Kate curled up fast asleep on his knee.

'I was trying not to disturb her,' he said. 'Will she wake up if I pick her up?'

'I don't think so. She's had a big day.' She had to smile at the pair of them together.

He scooped Kate up into his arms and carried her into her bedroom. Elizabeth turned down the covers and he slid her gently under them. Stirring slightly in her sleep, Kate turned over and smiled, eyes closed.

'She smiles in her sleep.' His face was turned away from her, fixed on Kate, like he could watch her forever. 'When she's happy. And that's most of the time.'

Bending over, he drew up the covers and kissed her on the cheek.

Elizabeth thought her heart would burst. Amazement, love and anger struggled for control.

They drank their coffee together, going over the plans for his house. All very official and professional. They discussed each part of the project and he signed off on them. Elizabeth drank in the image of his long legs crossed in front of him, his tapered fingers pointing out the various drawings and figures, his wide smile all the way from his crinkled eyes to his full lips.

Shaking herself, she gathered the papers and assured him she would get back with dates from the contractors in the next week.

'So how about tomorrow? Would you like to go out?' Elizabeth was trying to get a word in, but he rushed on. 'I thought we might go to El Cabalo Blanco. See the Spanish riding horses. I thought Kate might like that. We could have a picnic. What do you think?'

She was thinking he was a schemer. Planning all this through her worrying week. 'Look Martin,' she said firmly, 'I appreciate what you're doing for Kate, but we don't need it. We're okay.'

'Well.' He took a deep breath, making the air around him tingle with suspicion. She raised her eyebrows, waiting for his excuse. 'The place has become a customer of mine and they've offered me some tickets. I've been thinking about taking my sister Julie's boys there when they come and stay. Thought we could try it out. You and Kate could be my guinea pigs.'

He was so humble, so sweet, so persuasive, so damn reasonable, what could she say? 'Okay. But,' her hand went up to stop any incipient celebration – unsure whether it would be him or herself. 'Kate's used to a quiet life. I don't want her depending on you too much for fun.' It sounded somehow wrong but it captured some of her meaning.

The wide smile was back. 'I promise we won't have too much fun. Hand on heart.' And he clapped his hand to his chest. *Whose heart?* Elizabeth wondered.

As Martin had predicted, they enjoyed the day. Kate declared the horses magnificent – a new word for her – and the owners showed their new supplier a great time. At the end of the day Martin carried an exhausted Kate, back to the car, draped like Raggedy-Anne doll over his shoulder.

'It was a great day. Thank you,' Elizabeth told him as they drove off.

'No. Thank *you*.' His eyes were fixed on the driveway, hands fixed to the wheel, heart fixed on his sleeve.

There were times Elizabeth thought he was perfect - so attentive, adventurous and adept at all sorts of things. There were times Elizabeth thought his presence was more about Kate than about her, but then she would catch his searching gaze on her. Like a shimmer on the moon, his expression would shift and point towards something that Kate was doing, and she'd wonder if she'd read his face right. After that first week he kept her informed about his doings. For five days he worked hard at his business in order to have weekends to spend as he liked. He would ask for approval to come on a Friday evening, and agreement for weekend fun.

He attended a local church on Sunday mornings, and he invited Kate and Elizabeth to come along. 'I'll think about it,' she promised him, struggling again with the pick-up-stick complications of their relationship. She and Annie had been regular members of the church in Cowra, Kate was baptised there as a baby and, as a toddler, enjoyed playgroup. Elizabeth still sent Christmas cards to some of her friends from the church. Her reluctance was not about atheism, or even agnosticism but about connection with Martin – a joke really because they were becoming more connected with every passing day.

It was like being on a dinky flying down a hill. Her feet were keeping up with the racing pedals and, at the same time, driving it faster and faster, gaining momentum, picking up speed, hurtling towards the finish. Totally out of control, she could justify everything they did together. Meals, movies, outings, his ongoing presence, his phone calls, his invasion of her brain, his domination of the conversation with her daughter. All perfectly reasonable.

Meantime the contractors were booked and the work started on his house. He gave Elizabeth a key so she could supervise and approve the various stages. Sensible Liz ticked all the boxes, made decisions about changes and generally used her professional expertise to turn the new section of the house into a home. On the other hand, that infatuated girl with the traitorous heart saw rooms as possible scenes in her own romance. Places they could be together, or spend time with Kate, or maybe raise a family.

Tracey came one day to see the nearly finished product and caught Elizabeth daydreaming in the family room. 'What's going on that wall,' she asked, pointing at the empty space where Elizabeth's gaze was transfixed.

'Family photos,' Elizabeth answered, without thinking.

Her eyebrows shot up. 'He has family?'

'Everyone has family,' sensible Liz was taking control of the conversation. 'I'm sure he'll find somebody to hang on the wall.'

Tracey's restraint was screaming, but she turned away without comment. As they walked out, she asked, 'What's Martin think about all of it?'

'The house?'

'What else?' Eyebrows up again and a quirk of the lips.

Elizabeth tried to steer the conversation around. 'He loves it. Very happy. Can't wait to invite his nephews to come and stay.'

'The ones whose pictures he's going to hang on the wall,' added Tracey helpfully.

Elizabeth narrowed her eyes and nodded.

Tracey smiled. 'You look happy too.'

And surprisingly, she was.

Chapter 16

The winter days lengthened into the warmer spring. By the time the fruit trees in Martin's garden were covered in blossom and bees, the dinky was going full tilt. He would come around several weekday evenings and spend most of the weekend at either their place or his. They had become a team.

One Tuesday lunch time Mrs. Phillips from the nursery school rang. 'I don't want to worry you,' she said, of course she did, Elizabeth thought – unfairly - 'but Kate hit a little boy.'

'That's dreadful.' There was a first for everything. 'I'll have to talk to her about keeping her hands to herself.'

'Well,' the teacher's smile was leaking through the phone, 'he did deserve it – kept going on about everybody having a daddy except Kate. He wouldn't leave her alone. Kate got very upset.'

It had come to this. What Annie had been so afraid of for her Kate. A cold hard lump congealed in Elizabeth's throat.

Mrs. Phillips filled the gap, 'Well, she did say sorry to the boy. Very generous, I thought, under the circumstances. I talked to Kate privately and she insisted somebody called Martin would be her daddy if she asked him and said *please*. Your daughter has lovely manners.'

'Thank you.' Elizabeth was on automatic, trying to process all this information. Rather hysterically she thought that Kate caught her manners from her mother.

'But that's not the real reason I rang you. It's very unlike her. I think she lost her temper because she is not well. She seems very sniffly and teary today and not herself. I thought you might like to come and pick her up early.'

Elizabeth dropped everything, told Tracey she would work from home, and drove the short distance to pick up the family prize-fighter. It must have been all of thirty seconds after she drove off that Kate fell asleep in the car. There was no more discussion on any of the events of her day, either fraught or friendly. Likewise, trying to have a sensible conversation with her over dinner about asking Martin to be her daddy, proved to be well-nigh impossible.

'You said if I said *please* then people would say *yes*.' Kate pushed her favourite scrambled eggs around the plate like a kindy kid in a sand pit, her fevered eyes bright with unshed tears.

'It's not something you should ask people.' Elizabeth doubted subtlety would work. 'Have a little bit of your egg.'

'Annie said if you don't ask, you don't know.' Kate picked up the tiniest crumb of egg on the tip of her spoon and put it in her mouth, looking like it was poison.

'There are some things we don't ask people,' Elizabeth decided to be more frank. 'Asking Martin to be your daddy is not something I want you to do. And,' sensible Liz was rapidly losing control of the situation, 'while we're at it, we don't hit people. Ever.'

Kate's whole body sank like a deflated balloon. Her nose ran. She dropped her spoon, pleated her skirt up to her wobbling little mouth and sobbed like her heart was breaking – Elizabeth's certainly was.

'I hate Justin,' she slobbered. 'He's so horrible to everybody. He calls Christopher rude names. And he said I was Christopher's girlfriend. And when I said I wasn't we were just good friends he said nobody would be my friend because I haven't got a daddy.'

By this stage Elizabeth could easily have got up, driven to Justin's house, punched him, and anybody related to him. Instead, she gathered Kate up in her arms. The little girl turned into her mother's shoulder, snot and tears soaking into her shirt. Elizabeth found they were not only her daughter's tears, but hers as well. As they calmed, she wiped Kate's nose and realised she was hot with fever.

'You don't have to eat the eggs. Would you like some juice?' she asked, getting out the children's aspirin at the same time.

Kate nodded.

'And off to bed, I think.'

The following morning, Kate seemed a little better but when her fairy pyjamas were pulled off, there were spots on her back. A quick call to Mrs. Phillips confirmed Elizabeth's suspicions. 'Chicken Pox, probably. You're the fourth mother today. No wonder the place's been a warzone.'

The doctor visited in the afternoon. There was not much to do. Aspirin for fever, calamine lotion to stop the itch and keep her warm and quiet. Any other problems and ring him again.

Tracey was kind as ever. She would bring work over, she said. Could she pick anything up from the shops. Her poor little pet, fancy getting the pox.

Elizabeth left a message for Martin on his answering machine.

And that was that. They hunkered down, Kate in her little nest on the lounge in front of the TV and Elizabeth over her workbench, planning what she could do from home. Kate was fast asleep so she turned off the show, made some tea and tried to focus on plans for a restoration job. It was going to be a long week or two.

Martin turned up at 5.30, a bag full of colouring books and pencils for Kate, and a bottle of wine, a cooked chicken and a bunch of daffodils for her mother. 'A pox on your house,' he laughed.

'Very funny. Have you had the chicken pox?' Elizabeth was glad to see him but irritated by his lack of sympathy.

'I must have,' he answered, 'I was a very sickly child.' He graced her with a naughty wink.

She gave up. 'Come in then. Martin's here,' she called to the invalid, 'with colouring in, and barbecue chicken for dinner.' That might cheer her up.

As he handed over the adult goodies, their hands touched and eyes met. Very slowly his smile turned more serious, a slight frown creased his brow, and he dipped his head. Their lips touched for the briefest of kisses and then away he fled, responding to Kate's call.

Elizabeth stood trembling, rooted to the spot. The imprint of his lips burned her mouth. She was back, spinning back to the beginning: before Kate, before Annie, before her flight, before she knew the terrible responsibility of love. Eventually sensible Liz kicked in.

'Why don't I cook some veges to go with the chicken.'

'Not pumpkin,' a little voice came back. 'Pumpkin makes me sick.'

'I'm sure it doesn't.' Martin's voice rumbled with supressed laughter.

'Yes, it does,' mother and daughter chorused. And Elizabeth was out of her trance and back to reality.

'No pumpkin for you, princess,' she told Kate, as she carried the bowl of daffodils into the room. 'Here's some sunshine for you, though.'

'Oh goody, daffodowndillies,' Kate answered in Annie-speak. 'Look mum, Martin brought me a puppy puppet.'

Elizabeth admired the toy and smiled at the giver.

'I figured if she had this on one hand it might stop her scratching,' he explained.

'Do puppies get chicken pops, mum?' Kate asked.

'No, darling, only people do.'

'That's good.' She turned to Martin, 'Will you read me *The Friendly Book*?' she asked.

'Certainly,' he answered. 'Your wish is my command.'

And Elizabeth left them to it.

Chapter 17

He came every evening that week, ringing first to see if they needed anything from the shops, bringing food, and supplies – and laughter and love. Counting spots with Kate was their nightly activity and it helped to work out when there were finally no new ones.

Tracey would also come over each evening and bring some work and pick up what was completed. Kate was often asleep by the time she came, but Tracey brought her gifts as well.

'This has got to stop,' Elizabeth told the two of them towards the end of the illness over a glass of wine. 'She's ready to draw up a list of demands.'

'For Christmas?' asked Tracey, frowning slightly.

Martin smiled knowingly. 'For now.'

'So, no more,' Elizabeth insisted. 'It's going to take her years to colour in all those books and all she does with the Barbies is take their clothes off. There's naked Barbies everywhere.'

'What a good idea,' said Tracey. 'Naturist Barbie. All you need are accessories.'

'What are you laughing at?' called Kate from her nest in front of the TV.

'You,' Martin rumbled back.

'I'm not funny,' she called back indignantly, and trotted out into the kitchen to join the party. 'Just spotty.' She held up her shirt.

'Your spots are much better.' Tracey was examining her torso. 'But don't pick at the scabs or you'll end up with scars like me.' She pulled up her shirt at the back and turned so Kate could see her childhood marks from chicken pox.

'Wow,' exclaimed Kate, 'they must have been big chickens.'

The three adults all fell about. 'You are funny, darling.' Elizabeth hugged her. 'And we all love you for it.'

Tim Tam in hand she trotted happily back to the TV. 'Funny,' Elizabeth remarked, 'she's lost her appetite for vegetables but not for Tim Tams.

Martin was fun and fair and firm with Kate and had looked after the pair so well while they were locked away. Staying late into the evening most nights, he and Elizabeth sat in companionable silence watching TV together, or chatting when there was nothing worth watching on the box.

She told him about Annie. She had to really, Kate spoke of Annie all the time. But Elizabeth felt she could trust him with these precious memories.

'No wonder I couldn't find you. I'm so glad you were safe and well looked after.'

He never asked about why she flew away, or why she was so determined to raise Kate herself, or why she had never told him he had a daughter.

With Kate now scabless and back at Pre-school, Elizabeth was working her socks off, if she'd been wearing them instead of pantyhose. Martin probably was sockless because he would ring in the evening, instead of visiting, and was working like a Trojan, he said, to catch up. She apologised for taking up his time. But he just laughed. 'My choice,' he replied.

Saturday dawned hot and bright and he offered to take them on a beach picnic down the coast. It was such a treat to get out of the house, even if the water was still cool. The three plunged in, Kate swinging between the adults like a crazy orangutan, Lady padding after them into the shallows, barking at the seagulls. They assured each other it was not at all cold, brrrrr, then settled for sandcastles, stick fetching, and sandwiches on the beach. After lunch Martin stretched out on his stomach, and was soon snoring away with his nose pressed into the beach towel, Lady laid out next to him. Elizabeth covered him with Kate's towel and got out her camera, taking shots of the rolling sea, Kate's constructions and Martin's sonorous form. Two hours later the afternoon was beginning to cool and she had Kate dressed again. She gently shook

Martin's shoulder. His eyes slowly opened. 'Darling Liz,' he said, half-asleep, reaching up, then recalled where he was and sat up. 'Sorry. I'm so sorry. Fancy sleeping through our picnic.'

'You snore,' said Kate, gracing him with her newest raise-one-eyebrow trick and patting Lady at the same time.

'No, I don't,' Martin said.

'Yes, you do.,' Elizabeth smiled.

'That's okay, we don't mind,' Kate assured him and moved in for a hug. She peered at his chest. 'You've got spots,' she said, knowingly.

His gaze fell towards his navel. 'Damn,' he murmured.

Elizabeth inspected his front and then turned him around to examine his back. 'And there's a couple on your back with blisters.'

'No wonder I've been feeling under the weather.'

'You need to go to bed,' said Kate, well informed on the medical implications.

'Yes, I do,' he said, and, with all his misery, winked at Elizabeth.

Ignoring was tricky with an attractive man in a swimming costume. Even a spotty one. But

Elizabeth did her best. She loaded up towels, bags, daughter and dog and drove back up the coast to her house. Martin assured her he was safe to make it back to his own home, it wasn't that far away. So she armed him with the rest of the calamine lotion and prescribed Aspirin and sent him home to bed.

Chapter 18

Kate and Elizabeth called over the next evening and, as she put her key in the slot, the door was opened by a tall grey-haired woman bearing a striking resemblance to Martin. Elizabeth froze in horror as Kate bounded up but she rushed past both women and flung her arms around Lady who was, Mrs. Fielding said afterwards, behaving in character and dogging her every step. 'Come in, come in, Martin was hoping you'd drop by.'

They trailed in, carrying their gifts. The house looked great. It had been finished some time before the pox struck. Yet she still had the key. 'Hang on to it,' Martin had said. 'In case I think of more things I want done.'

Mrs Fielding relieved them of their parcels, 'Come in and see the spotty man,' she said, with that same half smile as her son. 'He can whinge to you now, instead of me.'

His spots were as spectacular and as numerous as the stars in the sky, from what was on show. He lay in just pyjama shorts. His mother offered to get a dressing gown but he shook his head. 'They've seen me like this before,' he assured her, 'we were at the beach yesterday when the spots came out.

Kate was next to him counting. 'I'm up to one hundred,' she said. 'But I don't know what comes next.'

'One hundred and one,' Mrs. Fielding said helpfully behind them. 'But you're going to need a lot more numbers than that.'

'I'm so sorry,' said Elizabeth with a guilty grin.

'Not your fault, I should've checked with Mum.'

And 'Mum' nodded sagely.

'Come and have a cup of tea, Liz,' she said, 'let's leave this poxy pair together.'

Kate said, 'Would you like me to read you a story, or would you like to play eye spy?' Elizabeth giggled. Kate knew her letters but they bore no resemblance to the words she wanted to use for eye spy. And poor Martin was at her complete mercy.

Martin's mother stayed for two weeks and Elizabeth and Kate rang, or dropped in for short visits. 'They say adults suffer more with childhood diseases and he was certainly very sick.' Mrs Fielding told Elizabeth on the phone one day. 'You know, he gave me the calamine lotion and one cotton bud and asked me to paint him. I suggested we needed a spray can. They're all over him. Even on the soles of his feet, between his toes, in his hair and in his mouth. It's a shame he never picked it up when his sister had it. But there you have it, he didn't.' At this moment Elizabeth realised how little she and Martin knew about each other.

What in heaven possessed her, she was never sure, but one Sunday morning in November she and Kate put on pretty dresses and took themselves off to Martin's church. It was an effort. Sensible Liz was screaming all the way about not getting too deep into this, both religion and relationship. *Well,* she responded mentally, as she pulled up in the parking lot, *you didn't mind when you went with Annie. Didn't hear you screaming when Kate was baptised.* That silenced sensible Liz temporarily. She sat in the car, hesitating, waiting for a sign of one sort or another.

A little voice in the back said, 'Are we going in?'

It nearly shook her out of indecision. 'I think so.'

'Well, come on,' said Kate firmly, flung her door open, hopped out, skipped up the stairs and disappeared through the door.

Is that sign enough for you? Annie whispered in her ear.

It was daunting. The little country church they had attended with Annie had been formal and traditional. This was none of that. Instead of hard pews there were comfortable, cushioned chairs, instead of well-known hymns there was modern music with guitars and drums, and the minister was not robed or scarfed but wore an open neck shirt and jeans. Elizabeth had entered another universe. However, the people were kind and caring. When they realised Kate was not in fact on her own but with her mother, they laughed and gave her information about the Sunday School, in case Kate wanted to go – which she did. So Elizabeth sat on her own, like an alien newly arrived on planet earth, and listened carefully.

There was a lavish morning tea after the service and various people came and introduced themselves and made her feel welcome. Kate skipped out from the children's room, her hands laden with craft activities, which she dutifully dumped in her mother's handbag and went off to cruise the morning tea table with the other children. The young minister came over and introduced himself and his wife. Elizabeth stayed around for about half an hour and then prised her daughter away from all her new friends and drove home, totally on overload. Not sure why. Nobody had asked how she came to be there, if she knew a member of the congregation or even if she lived nearby. They were the least nosy congregation she had ever met. Annie would have been disgusted. She would have had all that out in thirty seconds.

Martin wasn't there. His name was on the prayer list and they prayed for him and for his recovery. Elizabeth rang him during the afternoon and his mother answered the phone.

'How's he going?'

'Much better, but he gets tired easily. He's asleep at present. Had to go into work yesterday morning and he's been tired all day today. That's why I came over, to make sure he ate and slept. But I'm off home soon. Why don't you ring him a bit later, he does look forward to your calls.'

As it transpired, Tracey visited and they were catching up on all sorts of things. By the time she left and Kate was in bed, it was past the time Elizabeth was comfortable to call.

That set the scene for the next week. Playing phone tag on answering machines, Elizabeth and Martin could not catch each other. His final message was that he was going to have to work on Saturday to make up some of his lost time. He was most apologetic and said to give Kate a big hug and kiss from him. What about her? Elizabeth thought. Sensible Liz was horrified.

When she passed on his affection to Kate, the girl demanded they visit him at church on Sunday. 'I've decided to follow Jesus.' She announced.

'Is that why you want to go to church?' Elizabeth asked, her stomach grinding.

Kate put her head to one side. 'A bit.'

Elizabeth's anger was rising like boiling milk. 'Did Martin tell you to do that?'

Kate shook her head. 'No. Nannie did.' She smiled and began to hum *Jesus Loves me this I know*.

And Elizabeth was back again, sitting with Nannie as she rocked Kate in her arms.

Kate put her face up for a kiss, and Elizabeth obliged.

'I like being loved,' Kate whispered in her mother's ear. Like a punctured balloon Elizabeth subsided and her anger evaporated.

'So do I,' she admitted and thought she had no idea what that really meant. 'How about we ask Martin if we can come for a swim,' she suggested. Kate had been having swimming lessons and had finally mastered floating on her back. She'd been dying to show off to Martin. Elizabeth left yet another message on his message bank offering to bring lunch and swimmers.

Chapter 19

Martin had his back turned to Kate and Elizabeth in church, talking to an elderly couple as they sat down beside him. Her training had paid off and Kate did not interrupt the conversation. Listening to his words made Elizabeth flush with guilt. He was telling them how much work he had to catch up on after being sick. The service began and he turned in his seat, ready to rise for the music, realised he had somebody next to him and looked down at Kate. Elizabeth knew from experience shock affects people in various ways. Getting a fright made her shake uncontrollably. Annie after her fall was pale as the white marble floor. Martin went bright red. Then his mouth wobbled. Tears formed in his eyes. His face split into the biggest smile ever. Kate slipped her hand into his as the first song began, and then Elizabeth felt her other hand take hers. Tears rolled down Martin's cheeks but he sang on as if his heart was pouring out with every word.

First thing on arrival at Martin's house, of course, was a swim, Kate insisted. Lots of back-floating was the order of the day, and Martin showed her how to hold her breath and put her face in the water. An expert on blowing bubbles under the water, Kate soon learned to take a few strokes face down, much to her and Martin's delight. Kate was eventually dragged out of the water, shivering 'I'mm .... not ... cold,' through blue lips. Wrapped in a thick towel and laid on a banana lounge in the sun she soon warmed up while Martin cooked steaks and sausages on his BBQ and Elizabeth fetched the salads.

'I'm a good, good swimmer,' Kate told Martin with a typical four-year-old lack of humility, sausage hovering in front of her lips.

He agreed, 'Yes, you are, and you can come and practise here any time.'

'Really?' She looked at her mother with a cheesy smile and mischief bubbling in her eyes.

What could Elizabeth say? 'Sometimes. Eat your lunch.'

'Can I practise some more after lunch?'

Martin raised his eyebrows, his head on one side, so like his daughter.

'Okay. If you eat enough lunch. But you have to wait for half an hour first.'

'Can I play with Lady?'

'After lunch,' Martin and Elizabeth answered together and then said, 'Snap.'

'I can play snap,' Kate replied, quick on the uptake.

And they all laughed.

'Let's finish lunch first,' said Martin.

Lunch, a long ball game with the dog, another endless swim and Kate and the dog were both snoozing. After the hot day, clouds were gathering in the south and a storm was rolling in with a promised southerly change. Still in her bikini, Elizabeth padded barefoot across the tiled kitchen floor. 'When she wakes up, I'd better take her home.'

She turned and Martin was standing in the veranda doorway, towel wrapped over his costume.

'I can't take much more of this, Liz.'

'More of what?' Electricity crackled in the blustery atmosphere and way-off thunder drummed. He put his hands on her bare midriff and all thoughts drained away. His warm bare chest was against her skin and she floated out of consciousness as his mouth came down. Persuasively, adoringly, consuming all. Her whole body knew its place. She was home. All the anxieties and griefs and disappointments of the years drained away. They fitted together like his body was her other half.

Slowly he pulled away.

'Liz. Darling. We have to get married. I can't stand to say goodnight one more time. I've been so patient, sweetheart. But being apart from you for that fortnight used up all my reserves.'

His warm mouth fell again and all the pent-up feelings poured from one to another, sweeping them into a whirlpool of desire.

Kate mumbled and turned on the lounge in her sleep and they snapped back to their senses.

Martin took Elizabeth's hand and led her out to the table under the shade of the awning. He went back inside and returned with two long drinks clinking with ice.

'She's still asleep, darling.'

Elizabeth nodded dumbly, words stopped up in her throat, then took a long slug of the icy fruit juice.

He took her hand in both of his, stroking her palm thoughtfully, looking into her eyes. 'I meant what I said. Please will you marry me.'

'You want to be Kate's daddy,' she said, a ray of sense making its way through the fog.

'Yes. But more than that I want to be your husband. I love Kate dearly – but I loved you first. And I still do. You'll always be first.'

Tears dribbled down her cheeks but he went on.

'That night you came back here, I could have locked you up and kept you with me forever. Probably been arrested,' he laughed shortly. 'You must have known once I saw you again, I couldn't let you go.'

'Not really.' She was bemused by this different sort of man.

'I don't just want an off again, on again relationship, I want to be together forever.'

'Men say that.' She wanted so much to be convinced.

'I mean it,' he pressed her hands. 'Come be my wife and share my life. I promise I will always love you with all of me.'

A spatter of rain and a thump of thunder and they moved back inside. Kate was awake on the lounge. 'Time to go home,' Elizabeth told Kate, 'I'll think about it,' she told Kate's father. And that was as much as she could muster. Her childhood training was too strong.

'Take as long as you like,' he kissed Kate, and then Elizabeth. 'I'll wait for you.'

And he did. Patiently, thoughtfully, supportively, he turned her around.

Chapter 20

What possessed her to say yes? Half awake, the question was rolling through Elizabeth's head like the summer southerly coming in. She'd been dreaming of home. That other place she'd once shared with her mother and stepfather. She could smell the Pine-O-Clean her mum used to clean up when her stepfather was drunk; hear them shouting through the closed door and pillow over her head; see the disappointment in her mother's eyes; feel her stepfather's arms around her in an apologetic hug; and taste the grief, bitter as bile on the tongue, of never being able to speak about him again. Her mother had even given away the dolls' house. *Was she going to repeat her mother's failures?*

Kate got to preschool, somehow.

Tracey looked up as Elizabeth slumped into the office. Head on one side, the boss waggled her eyebrows, pursed her lips and said, 'Let me get out the Earl Grey.'

'I'm fine.'

Eye rolling was Tracey's speciality and she delivered the full treatment. 'Come on, tell big sis.' Drawing Elizabeth out of her chair and into the kitchenette, kettle was put on to boil and cottage teapot pulled off the shelf. 'Work can wait.'

'I'm getting married,' Elizabeth exploded as Tracey poured the boiling water over the tea leaves.

'Congratulations.' Her boss was studiously staring into the pot. 'To whom?'

'To whom?' There was definitely an echo in the room. 'Martin, *whom* else?'

'Just checking.' Tracey took two white, bone-china teacups from the cupboard and carried them back into the office, returning for the cottage teapot. Elizabeth followed her back and forth like Lady followed Martin.

'So,' she sipped thoughtfully at her tea. 'Why the panic?'

And for the life of her, Elizabeth could find no answer.

'Are you pregnant again?'

'No.' A wave of anger rose somersaulted through Elizabeth's gut. 'Why would you ask me that?'

'I thought you might be getting married because you had to. I mean, I'm sure it wasn't easy with Kate on your own. And you and Martin have been pretty well inseparable since you did his project. It's natural, isn't it?'

'Is it?'

'Yes,' said Tracey baldly.

'Then how come you're not married?'

The boss lady stretched back in her chair and stared out the window, her head slowly rolling from side to side. 'I've made some very poor choices in men. And most of them told me afterwards they already had wives.' She took a deep swig. 'To be honest, some did before.'

'See, that's what I mean. How can you depend on a man?'

Blank silence. The tea in the pot grew cold as Elizabeth's heart.

'You've been going to church, haven't you?' Tracey finally asked.

Elizabeth nodded, looking confused.

'Aren't you supposed to trust God to look after you if you believe?'

How did Tracey know that? 'I guess. Maybe I'm not used to being looked after. I'm usually the one who does the caring. I find it hard to trust.' And there it was. The worm at the centre of the apple. Elizabeth did love Martin. But he was unrecognisable because she had no model to hold him against, no concept of his motives, no way of understanding his love.

Tracey broke into this contemplation 'What about me? I look after you. Don't you trust me?'

Elizabeth nodded.

'Will you take my advice as your big sister?'

Elizabeth was nodding and waving around like a demented puppet and Tracey waited. Her advice had held good so far. It was obvious she loved the pair of them like family. And she was right, she had cared for them both deeply and dependably.

'Yes,' Elizabeth finally said, 'yes I will.'

'Do you love him?'

Tears coursed down her cheeks and her head bobbed up and down.

'Then marry him.' An enormous sigh came out of Tracey's mouth. 'We don't get that many chances in life and he's your best. I've never seen a man so besotted with a woman.'

A huge laugh exploded out Elizabeth's mouth and nose, spraying tea onto the desk. 'Besotted?'

Tracey nodded, eyes twinkling and held out her hanky.

Elizabeth blew her nose hard.

'But talk to him.' Tracey patted her hand. 'Tell him your fears. Don't lock yourself away. Tell him about your mum. And your stepdad. And - don't hold back.'

A sobbing sigh escaped Elizabeth.

'And, as you're going to need a maid of honour, I'm your girl. We can go dress shopping together. Kate'll love that.' Winking, she rose, took the teapot back out to the kitchenette, boiled the kettle and made fresh tea. 'Back to work,' she said, knowing that not much work was going to happen.

Elizabeth did have a talk with Martin. And many more besides. She could only say a little at a time. He accepted that she had problems with trusting. God had his back, he told her, he had put his trust in the Almighty sometime after Elizabeth vanished. The guilt drove him to find solace at church and into the arms of Jesus. Her heart sank when she realised how she had let him down. In her mother's world men were strong and there to protect women. Martin taught her that both had strengths and fragilities – and needed to look after each other.

Tracey urged her to take some time off to prepare so she finally turned to Sandi, the minister's wife, for advice. In a local café on a weekday morning Elizabeth sat down with her to pick her brains about marriage.

'I'm no expert,' Sandi said, 'Steven and I have our good days and bad days.'

'Do you get into trouble a lot?' Elizabeth asked.

Sandi's eyes widened and then she blinked twice. 'No more than he does.' With a firm nod.

'Who from?'

'Me, of course.'

Elizabeth was confused. 'Why?'

'Nothing serious really, he just goes off into his own little world and forgets us. We're a team but sometimes I have to remind him he has a family as well as a congregation.'

'Oh.' *A team,* that was a surprise. 'What's he do after that?' This was foreign ground.

'Usually laughs. Apologises. Tries to explain. Gives me a big hug and a kiss. Says he'll do better next time.' Sandi raised ironic eyebrows.

'And does he?'

'Sometimes.' She grinned. 'Well, mostly.'

'Does that,' Elizabeth hesitated, trying to grasp the thoughts flashing through her brain, '… come between you?'

'Not really,' Sandi patted her hand and she flinched. 'He knows I love him, and I know he loves me, and neither of us is perfect. Just forgiven. So, we forgive each other.'

The idea of forgiveness in marriage was foreign. Elizabeth told Sandi all about her mother and father and stepfather. In that quiet café the two women shared several pots of tea and while Elizabeth poured the bitter brew of her mother's story out to her new friend in the hope that she could learn to be different.

'Does Martin know all this?' Sandi asked.

'Some of it.'

She nodded slightly and then took Elizabeth's hand in both of hers. This time it felt good. Her hands were firm and warm and slightly pudgy, comforting and steadfast. 'Have you asked God to help you?'

'I don't know how.' The truth, as well.

'Let me pray for you now. And, if you want to, you can echo my words to God in your heart.' And she did. She asked Jesus to come into Elizabeth's life, to change her heart and still her fears. Those words sliced through the fibres of her flesh, to the rooms of her heart. It was like the world stopped as Sandi spoke and there was security and love and a future.

'Does this mean I'm a Christian?' Elizabeth asked. Kate would want to know.

'A Christian is a person who follows Jesus. So yes.'

'I don't think I'm good enough.' Elizabeth reclaimed her hands and took another mouthful of her rapidly cooling tea.

'Me neither.' Sandi smiled from one side of her mouth. 'Nobody is. As I said, we're not perfect, just forgiven.'

'Can you help me understand how to have a happy marriage?'

'I'll do my best,' she raised her eyebrows, 'but don't expect to come into my house and find a Stepford Wife, because I'm not. As I said, nobody's perfect.'

Elizabeth found herself laughing. 'I read that book and it was so creepy.'

Sandi bared her clenched teeth and her head nodded in agreement.

'Thank you,' said Elizabeth

'Now we've discussed the marriage, which is the most important thing,' she winked, 'let's talk about the wedding. I do love a wedding. Can I do the flowers?'

It was a simple ceremony. At their request, Elizabeth and Martin were married during the church service on a Sunday morning. The wedding dress was a waltz-length cream silk and Tracey looked wonderful in a turquoise pants suit. Of course, the star of the day was Kate. She chose an aqua frilly frock, because it looked like a mermaid dress, and carried matching red roses to the bride. Mother and daughter walked down the aisle hand in hand. 'I'm not giving you away, mummy,' she declared gravely before they stepped off. 'We're going to welcome Martin to our family together.' And they did.

Afterwards the congregation laid on a scrumptious morning tea complete with a wedding cake. Martin booked a late lunch at a local restaurant for family and close friends. John and Janet came from Cowra.

'Wouldn't miss it,' John stated at lunch. 'Now I see why I didn't make the grade,' wagging his head in Martin's direction. Janet thumped him playfully in the arm. 'Does he like your driving? Do you find enough pot-holes in the road here?' Elizabeth thumped him on the other arm this time and they were all laughing. Maybe the bride did have family.

And then there were Martin's mum and dad. 'Always wanted a granddaughter,' his father said. 'And you two are so welcome in our family.'

'I knew when you visited him with the pox.' His mother was nodding wisely, 'Nobody does that without love.'

Kate was having fun getting to know her boy cousins.

'Better go and rescue her,' said Grandpa, 'those boys get up to all sorts.'

There were no long speeches at church, just Kate thanking God for family and friends and food like they did on *Romper Room*, and Martin quietly raising his glass to his bride and introducing her as Mrs. Fielding.

It was perfect.

Sandi and Steven offered to have Kate while the couple had a short honeymoon on the Barrier Reef. 'Can Lady come too?' Kate wheedled Sandi.

'Sure,' her new friend replied, 'our cat loves a challenge.'

Green Island was beautiful. The colours were so amazing, Elizabeth wanted to come back and redecorate the kitchen in turquoise, green and sand. Martin laughed, and wondered out loud what he had got himself into. He taught her to snorkel and they spent hours out in the crystal-clear waters, floating over coral reefs like rainbow gardens, with flotillas of fish weaving in and out. Days were hot but tempered by a cooling sea breeze and nights were warm. They found each other there in a way Elizabeth had never imagined. Talked about intimacy and then practised it. No longer was this an experiment, or a brief blush of passion, or a passing fling. They fell into each other's arms each night as if their bodies belonged together. Because they did.

Sandi brought Kate out to the airport to pick them up and she raced towards them as they came out into the main hall screaming, 'Mum ... Dad ... Welcome ... Home.' And grabbed them both around the knees as if they'd been away for a year rather than a week.

'How's she been?' Elizabeth whispered over her head to Sandi.

'Perfect,' she replied. 'Happy.'

'How's the dog?' asked Martin with a cheesy grin.

'Okay,' said Sandi. 'The score's cat five, dog nil. I think Lady'll be glad to get home.'

The two women watched Kate and Martin stride off towards the luggage hall, arms swinging, Kate chattering away.

'Me too,' Elizabeth said, realising that home was wherever these two dear people were.

Chapter 21

Eighteen months after their wedding, the twins were born. Identical boys, what a handful. This time Martin was by Elizabeth's side throughout the labour and birth and continued to care for everyone during their early days. He would rouse Elizabeth in the night to feed them and wash all the nappies before work every morning.

Kate loved to tell the boys what to do, not bossy, just helpful. Her faith grew all the time and she was a conscientious and kind student, often chosen for citizenship awards in primary school.

The telling moment came when the Family Life Movement visited to her school for a mother and daughter evening to educate the girls about their bodies.

'Any questions?' Elizabeth asked her bravely as they pulled up in the driveway at home, expecting the worst.

Kate puckered her lips together in concentration, choosing words carefully. 'I know that Martin's my daddy because we chose him, but now I know how babies are made, Mum. Who made me with you?'

Like a drowning woman on a life raft, Elizabeth gripped the steering wheel, feeling numb with her daughter's practical application of all that information.

'It was Martin,' she choked out. 'We were …' she was struggling to find the words 'together … before I went to Annie's house. You are our child.'

The passenger door flew open and Kate raced up the path, threw open the front door, and leaped into Martin's waiting arms.

'You're my daddy, you're my daddy,' she was yelling.

'Of course, I am,' he laughed.

'My whole daddy, I mean,' her arms tight around his neck.

He was looking at Elizabeth over her head, his eyebrows nearly to his hairline.

'She asked,' she shrugged.

He shooed Kate towards her bedroom to get changed and brush her teeth before bed. 'Good. She needed to know. Are you okay?' He was looking back at Elizabeth.

'Better than that.' She was wiping the tears off her cheeks. 'God has been so good to me.' And she held his beloved face between her hands and kissed him long and strong.

'And me,' he answered as he came up for air.

'Me too,' said a small lady-like voice next to them, 'Group hug?'

Of course.

Epilogue

April 1987

Elizabeth's daughter reads in her soft, lilting voice. 'Annie May Webster, relict of August James Webster. Born 1890 died 1980 R.I.P.' Flooding back are warm memories of this place - a gentle practical love given by the soul whose body lays quietly there beneath the earth. 'What's relict mean, Mum? and R.I.P?'

They stand in the graveyard, Elizabeth and Kate, arms about each other. Her bright hair reflects her mother's in the rosy light. They soak up the last, long warmth of the sun that is lowering in the western sky. A cooling autumn breeze plays along the grey-green grass beyond the gravestones and ripples through their hair throwing sparks of burgundy and bronze. The sliding shadows of tall gums spear the earth.

From far away Elizabeth returns and squeezes her daughter's shoulder, daily closer to her own. 'Relict means she survived her husband. You know, Kate, Nannie lived far longer without Gus than she did with him.' And as an afterthought, 'R.I.P. means Rest in Peace.' Kate nods solemnly but in empathy.

Peace had been Annie's gift - peace and wisdom, and a haven to bear Kate.

Well Nannie, what do you think of her now?

Not bad, returns the smiling echo, *Pass with a push* - the kind laughter.

Elizabeth and her tall silent daughter are becalmed, caught in distant memory. Their gaze passes over the bush cemetery, beyond to dry paddocks and the fringe of gums and dappled hills etched in afterglow. Shadows patchwork the earth and a ghost of a breeze whispers in the stems of raw-silk grass. *She's lovely, my lovely, my lovely*....... She shuts her eyes and there is Annie, baby Kate against her breast, crooning.

'Here come our men... MUM!'

Elizabeth's eyes snap open.

Across the graveyard they lope, howling like wolves.

'Dad's a wolf,' yells Tom 'and we're his cubs,' finishes his bookend brother Simon. This twin-talk. amuses the whole family, but not so much their teachers.

'Leader of the Pack.' Their dark-haired father winks, his eyes like deep forest pools, shifting constantly between grey and green.

'No respect for the dead.' Wouldn't that make Annie laugh. Respect me now, she'd say, don't wait 'til I'm dead.

Her man stands behind her and pulls Elizabeth's stout body against his firm one, warm from running with their boys. 'She's here, is she, my love?' gently, sympathetically, 'I wish I'd known her.' *So do I*, Elizabeth thinks.

Turning from the past, she takes the twins' hands and leads them across the graveyard, through the old wrought-iron gate, back to the car. She needs to put this world in the past where it belongs. Juggling the twins' unanswerable questions, she is beset by images of the past. Cloaked in evening, the field of the dead dims, the distant hills marked by a molten gold line. The sky turns delft blue and the new child stirs within her swollen form, a joyous anticipation of what was still to be.

A pool of light spills out from the motel into the quiet country road. Combed, clean, and tidy, the children actually manage to walk across the lamplit parking lot to the adjoining restaurant without shouting or falling over each other. As everyone sits down, ladylike Kate pretends she doesn't know them, head buried in the menu. The boisterous pair insist on telling their best jokes to anyone – and everyone. The waitress laughs so much it infects their sister. 'Tell us a story, dad, about when you were a kid.' One of them says. And so the night goes on with Elizabeth joining the jollity of his remembered childhood while inside her memories fracture and creep faraway.

The large room is filled with the quiet sound of heavy, slow breathing as she lays wide-eyed in a shaft of moonlight. The path it cuts through midnight takes her back to an older time, where even her beloved cannot trespass, back through the past to the beginning.

Elizabeth can feel her body slackening and her mind roaming into sleep. The rhythm of heavy breathing soothes her even as this new life stirs in her womb where first she felt Kate quickening. They will visit Annie's family and John and Janet tomorrow, laugh at old times, Annie's words rich in their mouths, her love full and strong in her hearts. Celebrate friends and family and love and life – and faith and trust. And praise God.

Acknowledgements

J ust before Easter, around forty years ago, I had such a vivid dream I hardly wanted to wake. Despite having four young children, and a busy family Easter, I spent every spare minute over the weekend writing it out in longhand on huge sheets of recycled A3 computer paper. I suspect my darling husband was as patient with me then, as he is now, because I got it all down. So first I would like to acknowledge my husband, Lyall Wood, and all his love and support, and also his terrific close-editing skills.

For many years I believed that a Christian romance would never be published, so the manuscript sat in a filing cabinet untouched. It was finally resurrected and reworked after I joined the Omega Writers Group. I would like to acknowledge that group and all their encouragement, and in particular, my dear Beta readers, Jenny Glazebrook and Jaye Cox.

I would also like to acknowledge Elizabeth Chapman who told me it had been written all those years ago 'for such a time as this' and accepted it for publication under D.O.L.L.

And, finally, and primarily, thanks to our Great God, who leads us on such big-picture adventures to His Glory.

D.O.L.L.

Daughters of Love & Light is a ministry hub for women and an independent publisher of Christian women's literature.

We believe in Christ-centred community, creativity, and calling.

Join the community
www.daughtersofloveandlight.com